DÉJÀ VU

THE NOVEL

AUDRIANA CRISTELLO

Copyright © 2025 by Audriana Cristello

All rights reserved.

No part of this publication may be reproduced, distributed, or transmitted in any form or by any means, including photocopying, recording, or other electronic or mechanical methods, without the prior written permission of the publisher, except in the case of brief quotations embodied in critical reviews and certain other noncommercial uses permitted by copyright law.

Déjà Vu is a work of fiction. While some real people, places, establishments, and historical events are referenced in this novel, they are used in a fictional context. The characters and their stories are products of the author's imagination. Incidents, dialogue, and characterizations of actual persons, living or dead, are either products of the author's imagination or are used fictitiously. Any other resemblance to actual persons, living or dead, events, or locales are entirely coincidental.

References to real people, businesses, establishments, and events are intended only to provide a sense of authenticity and are used fictitiously. No portrayal of any real person is intended to represent their actual conduct, statements, or characteristics.

Cover design by Dân Toulet

First Edition: April 2025

ISBN: 979-10-976356-0-2 (paperback)
ISBN: 979-10-976356-1-9 (ebook)

Published independently
www.audrianacristello.com

For Dân. My husband. My soulmate.

Page 204 may live within this book now, but these promises and truths were first whispered between us. In giving my words to Matilda, I've found yet another way to devote myself to you, across time, across pages, across lives. ***Je t'aime pour toujours.***

Foreword

—

The architecture of our lives is built choice by choice, fear by fear, love by love. We construct walls believing they protect us, only to find ourselves imprisoned within them. We choose solitude thinking it preserves our freedom, only to discover a different kind of confinement. Some learn this wisdom too late, watching their possibilities crash against reality. Others receive the rarest gift—another chance, an opportunity to choose differently, to break the patterns that kept us running in circles. This story lives in that space between fate and choice.

While it reads like a biography—intimate and raw—it's a work of fiction that blurs the line between what's real and what's imagined. In this cosmic mercy lies the most profound truth: that we are not completed by achievement or acclaim, but by the courage to let ourselves be truly known, truly loved. And within that braveness, ensuring we don't disappear—we finally begin to exist.

1

June

I was born in June of 1940 to Patricia and Jim Eldridge. It was far from a modest hospital. When I was old enough to understand my mother's interactions with the working class and the consequences, I imagined her asking to change hospital rooms five times. I was born into a world of privilege and expectation.

My father, an overtaker of the industry with an office overlooking Central Park, cast a long shadow over my childhood. His confidence only skyrocketed once he set foot on Wall Street. In the '60s, Wall Street was expanding. With stocks on the rise after World War II and advancements in technology, our family became, to me, unbearably successful. His world was one of carefully cultivated connections and overpriced suits. From an early age, I was groomed to follow in his footsteps, to become the son he never had in a daughter's body.

I'd often sneak into my father's study, "off-limits" territory. I was searching for any trace of his personality within those cherry wood paneled walls. However, each time I would visit the same books he kept for show: Rimbaud, Blake, Baudelaire. He was a collector, not a reader. Much like he was a businessman, not an involved father.

As I entered my teens, I played the part expected of my parents. I dated the sons of my father's colleagues, wore the right clothes, said the right things. But beneath the veneer of the perfect daughter, I was suffocating. I had a rebellion boiling in my blood and no amount of my mother polishing my attitude could extinguish that.

Soon after, it was the early '60s. I was in my early twenties and the path my father had paved for me—a respectable marriage, a position in the family business—stretched out before me like a prison sentence. My mother wanted what my father wanted. She never seemed to have much of an opinion. She raised me to smile and importantly, not do anything that could embarrass our family or cost my father a big deal at work.

I had a double life. By night, I'd sneak out of my parents' penthouse on the Upper East Side. I'd strip off the designer dress that magically found its way into my closet every week and trade it for a fur, mini dress, and knee-high boots. I was unrecognizable by the time I added winged eyeliner and tossed my hair around.

DÉJÀ VU

Cafe Wha? in the Village became my second home. I'd nurse a single cup of coffee for hours. I still remember the first time I saw Bob Dylan. It was around June of 1962. He had just put out his first album. I was twenty-two years old. He said I had some kind of magic in my eyes. I'd never felt sexier. I thanked him and wished him success in his upcoming album. He gave a nodding smile and brushed past me. I had needed an electric compliment like that after the painfully boring dates my father organized. The magic he mentioned, however, what was it? I assumed it was the rebellion radiating in my pupils. Whatever he saw in me that night, it stayed with me my entire life. Whether it was Bob Dylan or the bartender, it encouraged me to stay. Perhaps I had finally discovered somewhere I could reside without any contact from my daytime life.

Over that year, record stores in the Village became my stomping ground too. The owner, Billy, began to recognize me as a familiar face after a few times. I'd bought plenty of vinyl records to match my quickly changing moods and overwhelming feelings of nostalgia. The Beatles' first album in '63 for dancing alone at night. I adored Lennon's voice, especially when he talked. It was uniquely him. I'd put on Ben E. King's "Stand By Me" when I took a bath to relax. And when I missed my grandmother and needed a good cry, I listened to Paul Anka's "I love Paris." She'd always hum the chorus when baking us croissants for *petit déjeuner*. Her dream was to take me to Paris for my 19th birthday, but she died unexpectedly in April of 1959. The trip was planned for June.

I think I have always been an incredibly nostalgic person, already anticipating the memory before the moment passes. The lines between the present and past blur. I'm not sure if I can consider it romantic or poetic, or if there's some underlying personality disorder.

I had met someone in a bar, The Fox, the night after I met Bob Dylan. It was a rather dingy underground bar, yet had this incredible energy to it. The walls were paneled in wood, leather booths, and velour embroidered chairs crowded the entire space.

Her name was Margot Leroy. She was the coolest girl I had ever met. French and effortlessly herself. She had the best fringe and style you'd ever seen. A modern muse. She had tightly curled hair. Dyed black to match the smoky eyeshadow (of course, she would say). She religiously wore her mini shorts with knee-high boots. Said she had to show off the long legs her *maman* gave her.

She took the stage, cigarette dangling from her lips. Her deep voice filled every corner of the room. She demanded everyone light up and listen when she sang. She moved to New York City because the music scene was really happening here. She didn't have anything tying her down to France.

Margot lived life unbound. She insisted that rules were made to be bent, if not broken entirely. "Live, *ma chérie*," she'd say, exhaling a cloud of smoke, "Because no one is going to do it for you." Margot was beyond her years, but more importantly, she was beyond society's expectations. She taught me to be the same. To be wild. Unapologetic.

Margot showed me possibilities. The allure of being desired but never possessed. Of being someone's fleeting muse, inspiring art before disappearing into the night. I had longed to teasingly toy with a man. Taking the cigarette from his lips, putting it out, leaning in and not kissing him. Telling him something infuriating like "Smoking isn't good for your health."

Although with time, I'd fallen off this horse and landed straight on my face. Margot was always right, after all. She always seemed to know better. Annoyingly brilliant, I'd call her.

I had asked the owner of The Fox to sing next Tuesday. A slow night for practice. Margot had him wrapped around her finger, so for her, he would say yes to nearly anything. Even allowing some young girl to sing in his bar who could potentially empty the place out. He insisted I would be great. I hoped he was right and not drunk off his own stock.

—

I was incredibly nervous, but put on a brave face. It was Tuesday night, and thankfully, there was a little crowd. The usuals. Drunk Dave manning the bar, practically hogging all the rum to himself. Sonny, the owner, looking like himself—relaxed. And at the bar, an eager to support Margot. The band wasn't there yet, which made me nervous. That and the twisted chords were like webs, threatening to tangle me on stage. My mind raced with the idea of falling, so I jumped on stage and began to untangle the mess from last night.

Margot walked in. I knew because I heard Sonny's voice increase by two octaves. He was always much more cheery when she was around. On his best behavior for a woman completely out of his league. She joined me and sat on the decaying wood stage.

"I told the boys last night to clean up after their gig," Margot said.

She was dating the lead singer, Rob, of last night's band. They were regulars here.

"It's okay. It's kind of calming my nerves. Better than biting my nails," I remarked. She smiled.

The band arrived ten minutes after I finished untangling all their chords. Their luck. Margot really was my fighter because she convinced her boyfriend's band to play with me. I only met them once and on my drunkest night, I spilled alcohol on his mother's satin tablecloth and danced barefoot on the dining table. The legs snapped right out from under me and the table was in pieces. I immediately fell out of my drunk fever. I rushed to grab any cash I had in my purse in hopes of forgiveness.

"Rob, I am so sorry. Please, take this. I will pay the damages. I don't know what's gotten into me," I cried.

He wasn't worried. Too stoned to be worried. The next day, however, he was pissed.

But Margot always had a way with people. She calmed him down quickly and found solutions. Rob's mother was a shark, a control freak. Her son being her only child, he carried lots of pressure on his shoulders to be a role model son. This accident would tarnish all his efforts to be crowned "best son ever."

I used the cash my mother gave me for the alterations of my dress for Rob's table. It was fixed the same day and his mother never knew about the party he threw. My mom never knew I altered all my clothing, so I could use the money for drinks at *Cafe Wha?* and vinyl records. Much like Rob's mother never knew her son had a growing drug addiction. Children can be better liars than adults, even when we've had less practice at it.

"June, you're on in 20," Sonny yelled from the bar. I nodded, nervously.

The next twenty minutes passed like two. I was quickly pulled out of a dazed stare to hear my name being called. By this time, a bigger audience had gathered. A group of friends about my age sat in the back booth, beers already in hand. Super cool-looking group.

"June, go ahead. It's time," Margot said.

She encouragingly pushed me and I took the stage. I held the microphone on the stand to steady myself. I wanted to faint already.

"Good evening," I said, my voice low. "I'm June."

I was trying to channel some kind of confidence by acting like this is not a big deal when in fact, my whole world could come crashing down if my performance doesn't go well.

"I'm gonna sing a few classics and something I wrote," I paused. "You guys all right with that?"

I had a sweet audience. The young group cheered and raised their glasses. My performance went just as I hoped it would. My set only lasted about 15 minutes. Sonny wasn't going to give me a normal time slot before he saw me sing.

I stepped off the stage, my heart still pounding. Margot rushed over, grinning proudly.

"You were a vision!" she promised, pulling me into a hug.

I felt like I had done something and yet, nothing at all. Everything came naturally. I'd never had a feeling like that. Complete rush and a sense of validation. I jumped off the stage.

"Come with me." Margot pulled at my arm. "You deserve a drink." We weaved through the tables to the bar where Sonny was pouring drinks. His eyes crinkled as he smiled at me.

"Not bad, kid. Not bad at all. Think you can do that again next week?"

My stomach flipped. "Really? You want me back?"

He shrugged, trying to play it cool. "Why not? Crowd seemed to like you, and I need a younger crowd in here. My regulars ought to die pretty soon, you know."

Margot squeezed my hand under the bar. "What does the rock star want? It's on me, *ma chérie*."

I hesitated. "Whiskey. Neat," I said, surprising myself.

Sonny raised an eyebrow, but poured without hesitation. It burned down my chest, but I liked it. Margot and I sat at a nearby booth for hours. We watched her boyfriend's band play after my set. She was so supportive. I loved that about her.

After that night, I went on to play every Tuesday. In the beginning, I was singing to men who needed their weekly scotch after work. Lonely businessmen. No wives, only assistants who file their papers wearing pencil skirts. They had the same arrogant yet lifeless eyes like my father's.

As time passed and the crowd's age started to diversify—Sonny was obliged to add me to another day. Friday night was my favorite. Six months into my weekly gigs, I had some regulars who came to see me. My name was spreading. "The girl who plays The Fox." I had a good thing going. Sonny was happy with the business and for me, I was happy to belong somewhere.

For months, I focused on my craft while taking business classes to please my family. I sang hundreds of gigs between 1963-64, each one feeling more and more natural. Often, Margot would join me on stage for a duo at the end of my set. With Margot, it was all good and fun.

She was working a lot those days at a small record label. She was a singer by blood but could inspire art like no other. Everyone loved her at the label. Singing with her was something we did to bond then.

2

June

It was October of 1964. I was one song into my set. A man, tall and lean with boots that fell heavy on the floor when he walked, sat at the booth against the wall. At this point, I could do my show mindlessly. My focus shifted entirely to him.

He didn't smile. His look didn't waver once, actually. He leaned forward, elbows on the table, hands clasped. He looked through his blue eyes to scan every inch of me. I couldn't shake the feeling that I was being evaluated, though, not admired. His gaze was giving me nothing of a clue. My skin prickled under my big fur coat when he finally seemed to fidget in his seat.

But he just sat there, unmoving, my entire set. He hadn't even ordered a drink.

As the band strummed their last chords, he abandoned his seat. His steps were loud and measured. He reached the edge of my stage and looked up at me, his blue eyes now close enough for me to see flecks of steel gray in them. His face was just inches from my knees. I could feel his warm breath through my tights.

Without a word, he extended his hand. His grip was firm as he helped me down from the stage, his hand dancing up my arm and onto my mid-back.

He leaned in close, his breath hot in my ear. He spoke in a gravelly accented voice.

"What are you drinking tonight?" His chin pointed down. Looking up from under his eyebrows, he said, "I only waited until the end of your show to ask you."

His words sent a shiver down my spine. Random, unexpected, and completely alluring. I found myself at a loss for words.

"Well, I guess it's only fair that I let you. Whiskey neat." It was a bold choice for someone who didn't often drink outside of wine, a celebratory cocktail, or beer.

At this moment, I felt so secure in myself as a musician and a woman. He guided me to the bar, his hand still resting on my back.

"She'll have a Whiskey neat. And I'll do the same. Thanks." His accent was kind. French like Margot's.

I sat on the barstool in front of Sonny. He seemed surprised to see me entertaining someone. I never put up with the men who approached me here; they were always the same—void of any real depth. Plus, they think because I'm a woman who sings in a bar, wears short skirts, and smears on dark eyeshadow, I could be a confidence boost to their crumbling self-esteem.

I faced the bar watching Sonny assemble our drinks—he was still standing, lingering behind me. A moment had passed, nothing but silence. I was in a trance watching the whiskey fill out the glasses. Just as my eyes glazed over, he spun my stool around so I'd face him. I was staring directly into his chest when I looked up to his eyes. He wore a simple white tee with silver necklaces. He was effortless in his style. T-shirt, black flare jeans, leather belt with matching boots, tousled hair. He was natural.

He took care of himself and prioritized the extra effort it takes to accessorize. He wore the biggest silver rings I'd ever seen and practically on every finger. His hair, soft and clean with the darkest brown color you'd swear was almost black.

The light reflected off the liquor bottles towering along the wall and shone into his eyes. I was swimming in blue. He propped one foot onto the footrest of my stool so he could lean in a little closer. Maybe I was drowning, not swimming. He smelled like citrusy oud. I found his smell comforting, masculine and sweet.

I let my coat fall off my shoulders as I crossed my legs. Time seemed to stand still. His eyes fell to my collarbone. He watched me so closely that he could most likely see the little beads of sweat resting on my skin.

"You don't want to know why I stayed?" He was smirking. He was a confident man, not an arrogant one.

"I presume it's because you're already falling in love with me," I said with a soft grin; however, my look didn't falter. I wanted to be seductive, not funny.

He reached for his drink, let out a little laugh and said, "Just maybe, but I need your name first."

I turned back to face the bar. I wanted him to spin my chair around again. "It's June," I said, turning back and tossing the hair off my shoulder, taking my glass.

"*À June et Claude alors*," he said, swinging my chair back around. His body was pressed against my legs.

I met my glass with his. "*Santé*," I said cheerfully, wincing as the whiskey went down. With Claude so close to me, everything in my body seemed heightened.

"Too strong?" he said.

"No, it's okay. *C'est bon pour la santé*," I said jokingly.

His eyes grew wide. "And she speaks French," he said. "How?"

I liked the feeling of impressing a stranger, but I think more specifically, him.

"My mother had me study French since I was twelve. She said it would open up more opportunities for me. France could be a new country for my dad to explore business in. I fell in and out of it, of course." I paused.

"Never did like doing what I'm told," I said.

He was such an active listener. He didn't even seem to notice the loud group of drunk guys storming in.

"I'd always admired the language, the fashion. And I made a friend who's from Paris. She teaches me. Margot is her name. She should be here soon actually. You guys should get along."

His smile softened. I loved that he cared about what I had to say.

"So tell me something, Claude." I tilted my head up to him. "Why did you stay?"

It felt warm in here suddenly. I pressed my glass against my skin, just below my ear. The coolness felt like an electric shock. Condensation tickled down my neck, and his eyes fell from mine to follow the beads of water tracing a path down my chest. I was always the type of girl to pour gasoline on fire, not water.

And I liked playing with him; I thought he looked good when he lost his train of thought.

"Well, I'm here for work. I'm a tour manager and the band was playing a couple gigs in the city. After the show tonight, I didn't want to go back to the hotel. I figured I would see what was going on in The Village."

My eyes grew twice the size. I was intrigued not only because I was a striving musician looking for her big break and he knew the right people, but more so because we had something major in common: music.

"Some guy was smoking in the entrance doorway and everyone could hear your voice from the street. I wanted to see the face behind the voice," he said, looking down at his feet.

When he spoke, it sounded like music. His accent and the way he searched for his words before he spoke were incredibly charming.

"And now that you have?" I spoke as if the words were smeared across my lips. I think I wanted him to kiss the words right off my tongue.

"Now that I have," he rested his hand on the bar inches from mine, "I think I need to know everything about you."

We laughed, but both knew it was a vulnerable and real moment. Wasn't just something that sounded good or something he could blurt out. He was an intentional man. What he wants, he goes after.

We talked through several drinks at the bar before moving into the corner booth. We shared our life stories without any hesitation. He knew all about my family dynamic and me, his. He had two other siblings, Léna and George. Léna was the oldest, George the middle, and Claude the youngest.

His mother didn't seem to care what career he chose, as long as it got him out of the house. His mother wanted to isolate herself in solitude and with Claude being the last kid to leave her house, she could have been happy with her son becoming a party clown for a living. He found the right connections early in his life. He was throwing down his drink at a bar in Paris and met a guy who knew this new band. They needed a tour manager. He didn't have any prior experience, but the guy trusted Claude immediately. He had the job that most people struggle to find for years. He insisted that it was pure luck, but he seemed to know every band's discography and his knowledge of sound equipment secured his place. He worked in a music store during his teenage years.

He was a rather awkward kid, studious and desperate for rapid change after high school. Adulthood, when he left his gray childhood home, was when he could finally breathe and see all the colors life had to offer. He came from pain, disappointment, and awkward phases. For such a smooth talker and effortless man, he could hide his past easily from others. Much like I hid myself—a runaway socialite daughter born to a tight-lipped mother and an exhausting father.

However, he showed no restraint in sparing me the details. He wanted me to know exactly where he came from. That there was more than what meets the eye.

He admitted, "June, I have to tell you. My last relationship ended because I never found the words with her, but with you, all I *do* is talk."

I smiled softly and twirled the cherry around in my cocktail. Before I could answer him with some sly comment, I heard a familiar voice entering the bar. Margot had a strong presence. You could hear her laugh from miles away.

She seemed to dance around the room, mingling with everyone in sight. Laughing with the group of junkies, twirling her way over to the bar to charm Sonny for her free drink of the night, placing a kiss on her boyfriend while he wraps up amp cords—she finally found herself in our booth, wondering who I looked so comfortable with.

"Don't tell me someone is quitting the band and you are taking auditions?" Margot sighed and plopped down heavily beside me. She wrapped her arm around me and placed a kiss on my cheek.

"Relax, Margot," I wiped her lipstick into my rosy blush to create a new color. "This is Claude. He is here for work. I met him after my show tonight."

Claude shifted in his seat before daring to speak. Margot was someone you needed to impress the first time around. Although she could get along with anyone, it was hard to win her trust.

They made a quick exchange in French. That was my cue to cut the tension, get another drink at the bar, and force them to find a real conversation. I wasn't sure why, but I wanted them to build a connection too. I knew he didn't live in New York, not even the country, but I wanted them to get along for the future.

By the time I came back with three fresh beers, Claude and Margot were laughing hysterically about their lives in Paris. The clueless tourists who barricaded the streets and the relentless attitudes of Parisians. They related stories of wandering aimlessly through Les Halles for fresh produce every weekend and sneaking into the red *métro* car, which at the time was reserved for the highest class.

"I would only sneak into first class on *métro ligne 6*. If I was going to risk trouble, I wanted to at least have the best view of *La Tour Eiffel*," Margot reasoned.

We all nodded in agreement and laughter. Margot seemed content with her reasoning and Claude, happy to have met someone with the same experiences. I thought about how surreal it must have been for them to connect about their former selves in a far-away place.

They told vibrant stories of Paris in the '60s. The rise of the French New Wave cinema that later spread to the USA, the togetherness during protest, a fair share of technological advancements too. For the creatives, it was a brilliant time to explore your passions. Many intellectuals, like writers, poets, musicians, fueled their ideas by coffee. The '60s was a flourishing era for café culture. At the time, Café de Flore was the spot for the existentialist writers like Simone de Beauvoir, while the American writers like Hemingway, took to Les Deux Magots next door. Margot dreamed of meeting Simone.

Claude and Margot got along perfectly. Their quick-witted humor matched, and their competitive streak to be right all the time was balanced by my peace-making tendencies. I learned a lot about him from all the interactions that night. He was kind-hearted with a notorious rebel streak.

Claude revealed that he adored the major French fashion houses. It was a time of pushing limits with new silhouettes and colors. Quite feminine.

"But you'll see one day—all women will run the world in suits. I think about my future wife and she's in a three-piece suit. She would be confident, unapologetically fashionable," he said. (Looking back now, Claude really did predict *Le Smoking* by Yves Saint Laurent before its debut in 1966.)

My eyes lit up when his did. I leaned forward, my elbows finding the table, now sticky with lime juice from prior cocktails. He adored fashion just like me. He opened his heart.

"That's really sweet," I said, my chin resting in my hand.

He shrugged. Margot's heel tapped my foot—like a signal or code to reach across the table, grab his face, kiss him, and reserve a wedding hall.

There was a moment where I felt a sort of hope. I didn't understand the sudden feeling at the time. It wasn't until the future that it made sense.

The crowd started to thin and Sonny called last orders. We said good night to Sonny and we all walked out in zigzagged lines. I nearly tripped over my feet on the sidewalk outside. I reached for Claude to steady myself. He was sturdy and I liked his broad shoulders, which reflected his strong personality. His eyes lingered on mine as we parted ways, a promise of something unspoken hanging in the air between us.

The next morning, I woke up in Margot's apartment, my head spinning from last night's alcohol. I rubbed my eyes with last night's mascara.

Margot was habitually the first person to wake, even after long nights. I found her already brewing coffee.

"Are you going to call him?" she asked, an eyebrow raised.

I shot her a look of confusion with red hangover eyes. She motioned toward my hand. I turned it over to reveal a phone number scratched into my palm with a ballpoint pen. The ink followed the lines of my hand, like a palm reader's map, leaving black, vein-like streaks all over. It was a miracle I could even make out what the numbers were.

I paced around the living room in last night's clothes. I stared at the number and then at the phone on the wall. I was trapped in this cycle for a few minutes. Margot was quiet—the kind of quiet when you have something to say. I turned to her as she settled into the couch with her coffee and opened the window for her morning cigarette.

"I don't know," I muttered. Margot rolled her eyes, taking a cigarette from her silver case.

"The man gave you his number. He wants you to call." She lit up, inhaling deeply before passing it to me. "Here. Dutch courage."

I reached for her cigarette. "I think you're meant to give me gin or something when you say that," I said, knowing I was just stalling. I took a long drag, feeling the nicotine steadying my nerves.

"Now call," she ordered, "before I do it for you."

I took a deep breath and began to turn the dial, wondering what his voice would sound like in the normality of the day. I waited for a telephone operator to direct me through.

He answered in the softest voice; I had woken him up. I apologized, but he told me he could hear a smile in my voice. I was happy to wake him so we could make a plan to see each other today. I suggested shopping secondhand in The Village. I knew a place, not too expensive, called Take It or Leave It. We agreed to meet in one hour.

Margot let me raid her closet for a black minidress and long necklaces to layer while she made me a cup of coffee. The next ten minutes turned into a shoe debate. In the end, I wore Margot's flat knee-high boots instead of mine.

I had two styles, and they changed by the day. Often, my mind was so pulled by both that my outfits would look like a mess of the two. I loved the dark style of a fur coat and heeled boots, which I alternated to when I sang. I'd taken on a mysterious and sexier shade of my personality. However, I loved the sheer dresses, fluidity, and French femininity of Jane Birkin too. I had a fringe cut, much like she had in the late '60s. Although, my teased-up hair and makeup were more Brigitte Bardot. I loved her messy yet carefully drawn-in black shadow and liner. I mimicked that for my daily look. Her natural confidence too—I tried to mimic that as well.

I threw on a vinyl from The Velvet Underground to fill the cavities of my mind that were prone to overthinking. I sat in front of the window with a compact mirror to redo my makeup.

I kissed Margot on the cheek, thanked her for the clothes and the pep talk. I threw on a pair of round sunglasses and left in a rush.

I didn't have time to overthink about my appearance, thankfully. I was quite insecure when direct sunlight hit my face. I had a few scars on my cheek from teenage years of imbalanced hormones and unnecessary family stress. "Battle scars," Margot always said. I never did learn how to change the negative outlook of my scars into a positive one. My mother used to say I had a galaxy of constellations for a face. For a fifteen-year-old, something like that can only be taken personally.

I still didn't know if she said that to attach something lighthearted to my misfortune or to make a mockery of me. If she meant to be cruel, I told myself it was only because she was so worn down by my father's constant judgment that she needed to diminish the other women in his life just to stand tall in comparison. It's not a justified reason, but it's a reason for the behavior.

I learned to be confident in the life I created outside my family, but would quickly wilt like a dehydrated flower in the face of my mother.

The few scars I had disappeared almost completely with age. Just a few divots under my cheekbones.

—

Claude arrived before me. I found him leaning against the window of the store, one leg propped on the stone ledge. He had the coolest style. He wore a pair of flared jeans complemented by an enormous silver-buckled belt, a wide-collared black t-shirt, and the same boots from last night. I crossed the street wrapped in his eye contact, anticipating a big embrace. His smile grew as his eyes fell down my body. He held me in his arms and placed a small kiss on the top of my head. Looking up at him, head just below his chin, I asked what he wanted to find today.

I told him I had a ritual for finding perfect clothes, like the fur coat I got for a few dollars when it would cost fifteen or twenty uptown. He trusted the process but wouldn't tell me what he wanted.

The music was loud, we sang obnoxiously, and the air was littered with the smell of vintage. We tore through racks of clothing to fuel our fashion show in the back of the store. I tore back the curtain of the dressing room. Claude sat next to the only mirror in the store. I pranced over to my reflection. It was a long, transparent dress done in white lace with bell-flared sleeves. I felt sexy, empowered to be standing nearly naked in the dress he chose.

He asked the owner to see a little gold choker necklace in the case too. He explained that it was 14k gold and originated from 1940s France. He had known the woman who wore it, a friend of his who had passed away somewhat recently and wanted it to be given to a set of young lovers. The owner smiled and said it was refreshing to see a couple so involved in each other's lives. We had no problem assuming the role the owner gave us; in fact, it came quite naturally for us to be so affectionate. I lifted my hair for Claude to clasp the necklace behind me. I looked at myself in the mirror. Claude stood unmoving. I turned to face him, the counter pressed coldly against my back. I was very aware now that I was wearing only a transparent dress with briefs underneath in broad daylight. He raised his hand to adjust the necklace and told the owner we'd take it. He kept it at the counter for us.

"You don't have to do that." I blushed, looking up into his eyes. He insisted. I didn't think he even knew the price.

There was a moment of complete calm while the owner searched for a mini satin bag to place it in. Time slowed. We both knew the severity of this gift; it was more than a kind or romantic gesture—this felt like a promise.

We assembled more outfits for each other over the next hour. I loved to play dress-up with him. I felt that any suppressed creativity I might have had could run wild, and he would never bat a judgmental eye.

He looked great in everything but decided on a camel-colored suede jacket and a gingham dress for his sister for when he returned to Paris.

"Take the white lace dress for our date tonight," he said, eyes steady beneath a slightly furrowed brow.

"I don't remember you asking if I already had plans tonight," I remarked, hands on my hips.

He asked if I had plans, stupidly. Of course I didn't, but it was in our nature to push each other's buttons.

We took a burger and shared fries at Ruby's diner after. I went to Ruby's often. Her food was homemade, cheap, and she let me control the jukebox. I liked to eat at the counter. The booths felt too antisocial, and I liked Ruby's staff. They were old with plenty of stories and lessons to pass on.

I grabbed Claude's hand and pulled him to the counter. It occurred to me that I had never come here with anyone before. Ruby's was my sacred secret and yet, it was natural to be here with Claude. I took my usual place.

"When you gonna record some of that music, June? I want to play it here so you become a big star," Ruby said, yelling over the coffee brewing.

I felt Claude's eyes begging me to match his gaze. I knew what he wanted to say. He told me he could arrange a free recording session if I wanted. A friend of his here in the city had a little studio and he owed him a favor.

I didn't know what to say, so I timidly shrugged and said nothing. He said we can revisit it later.

We talked through many topics our entire meal: our childhoods, passion, early traumas, the big questions that haunt human existence, our values, love.

I craved human interaction like this, I told him. Being completely untethered to a filter. Everything we said, we said with our chests, even the ugly truths of life; we were honest and found agreement. We talked about each topic as if it was us who will face these situations one day, forgetting that we were merely two strangers who met only last night.

If we had kids, he told me, we should only have them if we are in a good place with ourselves, individually and as a couple. Financially too, of course. We wanted to raise fully developed children with two parents who are present and capable of giving their all. We didn't want our children to feel like an afterthought or inconvenience, like we often were.

He spoke about passion like a poet. We agreed that we couldn't live without it in some form. Physical passion, passion in our work, even for the everyday mundane.

"If we don't have passion, we risk sleepwalking through our lives," he said. "Which is why I wasted no time in asking you on a date tonight."

I agreed with a little nod and smile, but became completely lost staring at his hands. I ached to reach out. I wanted to wrap my hands around his, like cradling a warm cup of coffee in winter.

Our hands were frustratingly, tantalizingly far apart. I met his eyes, silently asking for an invitation. He reached across the table and engulfed my hands in his.

"Another thing, don't think too much," he said, grinning.

"Tonight," I said. "Pure instinct. No overthinking, I promise."

I shifted in my seat, tightly crossing my legs. I had a new confidence to prove. I knew I was safe to let my guard down, to act on my thoughts and desires with him.

—

He had called Margot's phone later to say he had made a sudden change of plans for our date and that I wouldn't be disappointed. He refused to tell me what surprise he had planned, but to wear the white dress I bought that day with the gold necklace. We agreed to meet at The Hotel Chelsea, where he was staying that week with the band he managed.

The Chelsea was a bohemian masterpiece—worn velvet furnishings and walls draped in textured tapestries. The air was thick with the scent of clove cigarettes and leather. Claude appeared from the stairwell, his eyes darting around the room to find me. The moment our eyes met, the air crackled with electricity. My heels created the perfect rhythm as I strutted toward him; he stood motionless. I adjusted the necklace he had gifted me just before approaching him.

Abandoning all restraint, I lunged forward and met his lips with a passionate kiss. His face was hot. I tangled my fingers in his hair while he pulled me close against him.

"No overthinking tonight, like you said," I purred, my lips just inches from his. "I promised."

His look of surprise quickly turned into animalistic desire, his fingers dug possessively into my waist. "Kiss me in the cab too?" he begged, his voice low and gravelly.

Claude hailed a car down and asked for 128 West 45th Street. The ride was a blur of sweaty kisses, car horns in the distance, and sharp turns causing us to fall into each other's embrace. Claude found his way to the high slit of my dress revealing my thigh; we said nothing, just watched in unison as his fingers danced along the exposed skin.

My body was trembling with anticipation. The taxi pulled over outside The Peppermint Lounge and I practically pulled him out of the cab.

The potent cocktails made us both reckless and uninhibited; our bodies out of control in the way we danced.

"You didn't ask why I changed our plans for tonight," he yelled over the music. We were in the back corner now, taking a breath.

DÉJÀ VU

Word around the hotel was that The Rolling Stones were meant to make an appearance that night. Claude wanted to test our luck.

And true to the rumors, it wasn't long before the arrival of Mick Jagger and the rest of the Rolling Stones. They brought an electric energy with them and it radiated throughout the room.

Later that night, Mick flashed a wild grin toward us. Mick had asked me for a dance. Claude, being the selfless and the confident man he was, displayed no hesitation in letting me out of his embrace. It was a once-in-a-lifetime moment and it was just that.

Mick threw me around the dance floor, nearly spinning me into the small groups of people huddled around. He was an energetic dancer, never taking a moment to breathe. Cameras flashed all around us and the crowd began to cheer us on. We danced freely, and without any care about how we looked. *I* was dancing with Mick Jagger.

The Rolling Stones had left an hour or two after that. We left shortly after them to find somewhere quiet to grab a bite to eat. We settled on a family-owned Italian place near The Hotel Chelsea called Pesto.

The restaurant was cluttered with dimly lit candles and old cooking books stacked in towering bookshelves. It was an intimate place, and the perfect change of pace we needed.

We were seated with white wine, olives, and bread. We recapped the events of the night over pasta. Our kiss in the lobby, though, topped dancing with Mick Jagger. He was shocked to hear that.

The waiter replaced our empty plates with a tiramisu to share. It was on the house and we devoured it in minutes. Reaching across the table for his hand, I gently traced my finger along the lines of his palm.

"You've been so generous to me," I said. I didn't understand how someone I've known for less than twenty-four hours could give me so much without anything expected in return. "What are you searching for?"

"You," he said.

My stomach turned inside out. The candlelight flickered across Claude's face. I swallowed hard, fighting the surge of emotions threatening to overwhelm me.

"How can you be so sure? We've known each other for such a short time," I questioned, even as my heart fluttered.

With a wry smile, he replied, "Tell me what you really want to say, June."

I leaned in, "You're right," I breathed out, my lips only inches from his. "I want you."

He began to laugh through a smile and captured my mouth in a soft, tender kiss. I melted into him, savoring the taste of espresso left on his lips.

"So," Claude whispered, his voice laced with desire, "Where do we go from here?"

Only a few moments following his obvious question, we asked for the bill. We hurried out into the night, hand in hand. We hailed a cab. Flustered with emotion and tension, we fled the backseat and pulled each other into the Hotel Chelsea.

We had to embrace the time we had because Claude would leave in only two days.

•••

We wish for our last moments alive to be with people we love and in a safe place. I was with someone I loved. The air was filled with his desperate cries for fate to spare our lives. I thought about the forensics team that would examine the car crash and find the imprints of my fingernails dug deeply into his hand. His breath caught in his throat as we watched our driver wrestle the steering wheel; it all felt wrong. I had thought about the possibility of dying with my loved one in a violent way before, imagining complete terror in our eyes. This wasn't a look of fear, but more of disappointment. We struggled for years on two separate continents, trying to make it work. We had finally been in the same place in our wildly changing lives then. I was 27 years old, Claude 28.

June Eldridge 1940 – 1967

Claude Beaumont 1939 –1967

3

Matilda

My seat was wedged between a businessman, eyes glossy and glued to his laptop, and an elderly woman clutching her rosary. The range of passengers struck me—one focused on the worldly, the other on the divine. There was a particular anonymity that came with air travel, and I sought comfort in it. Strangers are willingly forced into a confined space with no choice but to breathe the same air, and even fall into deep sleeps, without ever truly connecting.

I gazed out the small oval window as the plane taxied down the runway. The sun was setting along the New York skyline. I was going to Paris. Alone. It was November of 1994. I was a fresh twenty years old at the time.

For years, I'd defined myself through the complexities of my last relationship and thought I deserved to be unhappy, tortured, and out of control. I had lost myself, completely. I had convinced myself I felt light on my feet, but I constantly dragged my heavy heart around; I was drained of all strength when we fought. That's the problem with people who harbor all your energy for themselves: you never find the willpower to leave.

I decided Paris was the perfect city to reconnect with myself. I planned to indulge in my passions: strolling through Rodin's sculptures and his garden, sipping an espresso while writing at Café de Flore like all our best writers in the 1960s.

The ground below had faded to a patchwork quilt of greens and browns. I read my magazines, mainly the latest issue of *Vogue*, and part of a novel.

I picked up my journal midway through the flight. I was holding onto a lot so I found it best to scribble my thoughts onto paper.

I liked to write. Poetry was an art form to me, one in which I could slow my rapid thoughts; fashion articles fed my external self-expression, while poetry nurtured the internal commotion I felt at the time. I never go back to revise any of my poems. It was pure instinct in the way the pen moved to, somehow, form elaborate sentences and words with weight.

You served me lies on a silver platter.
I was caught up in the divine presentation that when the silver tray was lifted, I nearly ignored the deceitful aftertaste that follows.

I was starving.
I indulged in the false stories you handfed me.

We all want love, but you had it with someone else. In our bed.

Matilda November

I drifted off to sleep, pen still in hand, but soon awoke to the pilot announcing we will land in fifteen minutes. Forgetfully, I rubbed my eyes, smearing mascara across my eyelids, then proceeded to fix my tired raccoon eyes.

We landed. The plane pulled into the gate as passengers clicked their seat belts off and threw them to the side, the metal clanging against the seat. An occurrence so normal, yet it almost seems scripted every time. The simplicity of human nature is fascinating because you never expect to notice something like that, but when you do, it's like observing the universal behaviors of humans as an alien.

I reunited with my suitcase. I had booked a driver to take me to the hotel. I splurged. It didn't feel right to find a cab on the street.

I scanned the room for the little sign with "Matilda" written on it. I found him and he helped me lift my luggage into the trunk. His name was Laurent. He was kind, talkative, and curious about life in New York.

"I want to sit in a café," he said. "No, a coffee shop you call it, and walk around Central Park."

He told me it was all he saw on television. He asked me lots of questions. Whether the western films he saw were accurate. If the Quarterback and Cheerleader really do win Prom Queen and King. If Americans eat fries and milkshakes at diners with waitresses wearing roller skates. I jotted down five *recent* films for him to watch.

We were five minutes from the hotel now. I booked a charming room on the island in Paris, Île Saint-Louis. It was lightly raining that morning. The lights towered over the bridge and bounced off the slick streets. Something felt oddly familiar, like a half-remembered dream.

The island was calm and residential. The hotel was called Hotel de Lutèce. It was nestled into the island and overlooked The Seine from just one street over. My room was the 12th of 23. Each room had its own charm and decor. My room was decorated in an olive green wallpaper with white flowers scattered onto each wall and my bed covered in pillows. I dropped my bag onto the red armchair in the corner. The upholstery looked tired and worn-out, but still had a coziness to it.

The hotel was built in 1700 and smelled like old books. In the lobby, a stone fireplace with a gorgeous wood mantel sat in the corner. I had the idea to bring a book and cozy up under a blanket near the fire. It was only November, but it had already been a rather cold year.

I unpacked immediately to feel settled. I hopped in the shower to wash off my travel day. I wrapped myself in the white robe hanging on the door. I quickly blow-dried my brown hair and styled it into bouncy curls. I loved the volume Cindy Crawford always had, so I mimicked that, throwing my wispy bangs up into rollers.

The bathroom was decorated in beautiful, hand-painted blue tiles. Baby blue like my eyes. The sink was small, but I loved the simplicity of it all. I balanced my makeup along the sides of the counter, hoping nothing would fall. I touched up with mascara and a merlot-tinted lip. I religiously used Chanel products to feel closer to fashion.

I dressed myself in a cream cashmere sweater paired with jeans and heeled boots. The '90s were a time to get back to the basics that just work. Quality over quantity and my wardrobe was my pride and joy. Cashmeres, tweeds, linens, pure cottons.

And I treated each clothing piece with respect and care. In my mind, these garments were once an idea in someone's head who later sat down with a sketch artist. After, that sketch falls into the hands of the teams who buy the materials, those who produce it, market it, etc. Then you have the team who allocates those pieces for specific locations with different climates and cultures with the help, of course, from those who study consumer behavior. Then, it is passed from delivery carriers into the hands of the stock manager in each boutique. Finally, it is the salespeople who sell the creation to the public.

It is not just a garment you wash and wear; it was once someone's thoughts run wild. And for that reason, I loved fashion, but just hadn't figured out where I belonged in the process yet.

Once I felt like myself again, I took a walk around Île Saint-Louis. The cobblestone streets glistened from the morning rain. Apartments with wrought-iron balconies and locals walking their dogs led me down the narrow streets.

The smell of fresh bread and pastries led me to a family-run *boulangerie*. I asked for a baguette and she suggested a *fromagerie* just a few shops down the street. I asked the *fromager* to surprise me; he wrapped up a sweet cheese, Saint-Nectaire. He held up a finger, indicating to wait here. He came back with prosciutto.

"*Ça va être bon, tout ça,*" he said. "I give you the prosciutto free, Madame."

I thanked him, feeling so much gratitude. His kindness really touched me. His name was Michel and he wore a tweed paperboy hat. Suited him well.

I found an empty bench overlooking the Seine and assembled my lunch. I watched Parisians hurry by, wondering about their lives, their troubles, and relationships. One could easily disappear here and become someone new entirely.

I'm a nostalgic, emotive person at heart. I was in Paris to experience the joy of my own solitude, but I was also grieving the loss of someone. However, through much time sitting, watching water splash along the banks, I realized that all I had truly lost was the idea of someone. As his behavior and under appreciation worsened, I had let him go naturally over time.

Lonely, I sat on the bench and wept. I cried into the hands he had forcefully pinned against the wall in a rage. I wiped tears from the eye he had bruised, swearing it was an accident and that he would stop drinking. I quickly raced back to the hotel for a shower, possessed by the obsessive thought that his touch was still laced in my skin. I scrubbed my thighs red with the hotel exfoliant and fell asleep in my robe after.

As evening approached, hunger led me to a small bistro on the corner. I found it endearing that the chalkboard menus were handwritten each morning. Inside, worn wooden tables topped with flickering candles cluttered the room; the walls were decorated with black-and-white photographs, presumably of the married couple who own the restaurant.

The waiter recommended the *confit de canard*. I'd never eaten duck before, but I loved to indulge in trying French cuisine. In honor of the dish, I traded white wine for red. I pinned my hair into a clip and dove into my meal.

Later that night, I curled up by the fireplace in the lobby. To my surprise, the hotel manager brought me a cup of hot chocolate and a silver bowl filled to the top with Chantilly. I was remarkably spoiled today by the kindness of others.

The next morning, I was greeted by the sun streaming through the lace curtains that hung over the small windows. I dragged myself out of bed to look out onto The Seine for confirmation that I really was in Paris. The morning light felt different, brighter than New York's, but still heavily polluted. At the time, Paris was a city full of cars. The worst in the world for congested traffic, but it was in my favor to see the positive in every situation.

I made a call down to Room Service for a *petit déjeuner*. I told myself that the time I have in Paris is about me. I would allow myself to indulge in finer things and feel good about feeling good.

I was caught brushing my teeth when I heard a light knock at the door. A mute old woman named Françoise arrived with a beautiful spread of colors on the table. She welcomed me into the lobby when I checked in yesterday. She shyly nodded, avoiding much eye contact when I thanked her.

I was left with an enormous table in such a small space. I had freshly squeezed orange juice, half a baguette with butter and strawberry jam, a flaky croissant and a much-needed cappuccino dusted with cinnamon. I lifted the cup to my lips, cradling its warmth in my hands. The morning was silent, but I felt a jolt of energy then. It was something unfamiliar—hope, maybe. I decided that I wouldn't run from my past, but to build the future I wanted. I pulled out the little notebook I'd bought in the airport and jotted down all my manifestations.

4

Matilda

Over the last four days, I experienced the complete cycle of acceptance. Denial: Purposely fell back asleep to avoid the loneliness of waking up alone. Anger: Burned the poem he wrote for me, the one I kept in my wallet for years. Depression: Cried holding the burnt shards of paper to my chest. Bargaining: Convinced myself that if I hadn't been so complicated, he wouldn't have looked elsewhere for love. And finally, Acceptance: The poem was shit and he will always be a violent, manipulative cheater.

If I wasn't dead asleep, I was overthinking. I called room service for practically every meal I ate, losing count of the bill I was running. However, I hadn't eaten much in reality. I slept through breakfast and lunch service so there wasn't much choice but to order from the dinner menu. I would order a variation of a sandwich and fries every evening. I did order a tiramisu last night once I reached the acceptance stage though.

The only person to see me those days was Françoise from Room Service, each time a bit relieved that I was eating. The Do Not Disturb sign hung on the door handle with purpose, like a guard dog. Each afternoon, the squeaky wheels of the cleaning cart would come to a stop outside my door, only to continue past seconds later.

This morning, however, I was greeted with the warmth of sunshine on my back. I pulled my lips into a smile. I rolled over, the duvet wrapped around my legs like a vine. I stayed curled up in bed for another half hour, but this time, not out of fear to start the day alone.

Françoise greeted me with a coffee and *pain au chocolat*. I savored it, letting the chocolate melt on my tongue. The coffee was strong. I doused the bitter taste with my nearly finished pastry.

That day, I decided to rejoin the outside world by visiting Le Musée Rodin in the seventh arrondissement. I chose a brown suede jacket, jeans, and a matching belt-and-boots combination. I tended to opt for an understated yet chic look. I connected with Parisian fashion in that sense, but stayed true to my New York roots. I felt like myself again.

I spent nearly one hour at The Rodin Museum. It was a place where beauty and pain coexisted in bronze and marble. I wandered through the garden, alternating between reading each plaque and sitting on a nearby bench to reflect on the sculptures that connected with me.

I spent the longest time observing *La Porte de l'Enfer,* translated to *The Gates of Hell*. Like a 3-D piece, each mini sculpture intertwined with each other in the door itself: angels, starving, thin humans, little babies at the base of the door, and *The Thinker* resting above those who climb their way up the door.

And just beside the towering door stood *Adam and Eve*—a shocking yet intentional message. Rodin constantly explored the line separating purity from evil, the givers from the takers.

He had spent thirty-seven years, on and off, creating this piece with his assistants. I was saddened to learn that he never saw the finished work before he died. Most horrifically, however, he often took credit for his assistants' work. My mood shifted after that.

Going inside, I stopped to examine *The Kiss* and fell into a trance, even after groups of tourists had already moved on. I learned this sculpture was never meant to be this big. It was originally created in miniature form for *The Gates of Hell.*

The couple, Paolo and Francesca, were caught in their embrace, killed by Francesca's husband and condemned to eternity in Hell. However, Rodin decided to remove it from the door because its freeing sensuality didn't share the same harmony as the rest. Later, he enlarged the sculpture into marble, following the French state's orders.

In a way, and I knew it was wrong, I liked the story. Witnessing my own version of cheating lovers, I found some peace in the consequences they received. It was wrong, but I thought Rodin might call it human nature.

—

From there, I let my feet carry me through the streets and *métro*, all the way to *La Tour Eiffel*. I didn't stay long to avoid the groups of tourists with no sense of direction. I broke away from the crowds in the garden and found a quiet spot on Rue de l'Université. At this time, it was not as popular and I had an incredible view. The Eiffel Tower stood proud, positioned in the center of two Haussmannian buildings. I admired the architectural beauty in each piece of wrought iron. I stood there, stunned, soaking in just how truly tall it was.

This felt like a picture-worthy moment. I bought an Olympus point-and-shoot film camera for this trip. It launched three years before in 1991. It was an anticipated release since '89, and I had waited patiently to get my hands on it. I ran into the center of the street to line up my shot.

For lunch, I ducked into a tiny French Bistro. I was influenced to try the *plat du jour*: Cordon Bleu and a side of roquette.

I spent some time wandering around Île de la Cité. I visited the Sainte-Chapelle. I didn't belong to a religion, but there was something about the stained glass windows and 13th-century moldings that posed the question of human creation. It demanded that you be a part of something bigger than just that moment. I thought back to Rodin.

Evening approached and I found myself back on Île Saint-Louis in the bistro that had comforted me on my first night. I chose a table outside, embracing the golden light peeking through the trees. Brown and orange leaves littered the ground lining The Seine—it was a perfect view.

The waiter recognized me, offering a gentle smile. I ordered the same dish as before, *confit de canard*. In hindsight, I should have ordered something different, but I followed my desires. I promised myself that.

That's when I saw him. His dark brown hair fell in soft waves, curling slightly around his ears. A few stray strands were tucked into the collar of his turtleneck sweater.

He sat a few tables away, devouring a book, his fork hovering halfway to his mouth. Something about him felt familiar—a pull, an inexplicable urge to know him. Our eyes met, and I quickly looked away.

I didn't speak to him that night. For three days, I returned to the bistro for dinner, choosing the same table, always hoping he'd be there. But he never was.

Then, on the fourth day, there he was again. Same table, same book. This time, I stood, my nerves on the rise, and walked toward him. I had my little excuse prepared for four days.

"Excuse me," I said. "Can I ask where you bought this book?"

We both looked down at the book. He had marked up the pages and littered all of the margins with his notes. I continued, "I haven't found an English bookstore and I finished my book last night."

I lied. I had more than half left to read, but I had to find an excuse that wouldn't draw me as insane or intrusive.

He looked up again, his beaming green eyes meeting mine. The connection I felt was immediate. It wasn't quite an overwhelming feeling of attraction, not exactly. It's true, he was beautiful, like a poem I'd write in a garden, but this felt more like a reunion.

"It's a bookstore just down the street, actually," he replied, his voice warm. "Do you have a pen?"

I ran back with my bag to find him ripping a piece of the napkin off. He asked me to sit with him while he wrote down the bookstore's name.

As I sat down, the energy shifted us, like the universe had reserved this moment for us, at this very place and time.

"I'm Matilda," I offered, my voice more confident than I actually felt.

"Yves," he replied, his smile reaching his eyes. "You live in Paris now?"

I shook my head, explaining briefly about my impromptu trip from New York. As we talked, I opened up and found a new way to talk about the breakup. No excuses, no pity and without regret. There was something about him that gave me peace, like confiding in an old friend instead of a stranger.

We discussed his book—a collection of Paul Éluard's poetry translated to English. He pulled the French version from his bag and explained that he marked the margins when he needed a translation and then consulted the French version. I said I was proud of him—an emotion usually reserved for people who know each other, or at least enough to understand that this took some courage. He thanked me with a soft grin.

A moment of silence passed between us, like a game of who gives up first and states the obvious.

"Have we met before?" He finally asked, unable to sit another second in silence.

My brows furrowed and I let out a loud breath. "I don't think so, but I know what you mean. There's something about you-."

He released an exasperated breath, interrupting my train of thought. "Exactly! I just can't put my fi– maybe I saw you already. Like in a museum or I passed you on the street."

We both shook our heads and agreed it was deeper than that.

As the evening grew darker, the bistro emptied. The waiter began stacking chairs, shooting us the "get lost" glances. We took the hint and continued our conversation with a walk along the Seine.

We talked about our dream lives, what our passions were at the time, our jobs and love for Paris.

The air was cool against my skin and I couldn't stop my teeth from chattering. Yves stopped straight in his tracks. He unraveled a scarf from his neck and placed it around mine. He joked that a big tough New York City girl with colder winters can't handle a walk along the water. It was refreshing to hear a true laugh—one that came from a real place of joy.

Yves told me about his work as an architect, taking on smaller projects in Paris for now, but with hopes to be a part of a larger project like designing office buildings or houses that pay big.

He was born in Paris to a father who was a painter and a mother who worked in immigration. Being from two different worlds, Yves explained, it wasn't always easy for his mother to abandon the rules and embrace a free spirit, like his father. As much as his father, Robert, was a perfectionist in his art; he liked to color outside the lines in his personal life. Barbara often felt embarrassed in his company at dinner parties. They divorced when Yves was ten years old.

He told me he wasn't a lucky man. He believed the good things in his life only stayed that way because he kept a close eye; otherwise, he feared they would turn bad if he let his guard down.

He said, however, that he kept a peaceful and pretty outlook of his parents. Yves had this way about him; he was strong by nature, and I had the impression that he always handled things right the first time. Like an old soul might.

I was once a girl trapped under the pressure and fear of becoming an afterthought. In my childhood, my mother never could open up to me. In an attempt to win her affection, I aced all my tests, never complained about my dinner, and I would reorganize my room and drag her to see it in hopes that she would crack a smile and tell me "good job." I was cracking under the pressure, and before I could resolve those traumas, I was thrown into womanhood where I kept myself in a relationship that made me feel like an afterthought.

We listened to each other struggle to find the right words, but we listened. It was simple: I understood him and he understood me.

As the evening progressed, I found myself drawn not just to his physical appearance, but to all the little mannerisms: the way he articulated the words he wasn't completely sure of and the little hand gestures that follow along in his stories.

We found ourselves at the lobby entrance of my little hotel. We stood together wrapping up the last of our conversation about Paris and my first impressions—a city that begs to be loved and to give love, but demands you be open to receive it.

We made a promise to see each other tomorrow evening. In French fashion, Yves initiated *la bise,* placing two light kisses on my cheeks. We parted ways, him walking slowly under the street lights. I watched him, almost wishing he'd come back. I turned toward the lobby.

"Matilda," he called. I stopped and turned in my tracks. He ran back to meet me face-to-face.

"Turn the heater on," he said, concern in his eyes. "It's very cold at night."

I looked down at my feet and said, "There's a small fireplace in my room, but I'm scared to light it."

He grinned and took the hint. He followed me through the lobby and into my room. I threw my jacket onto the armchair and said, "Listen, I know what it sounds like. A woman invites the beautiful foreign man into her room to light a fire."

He nodded his head and started to laugh. "Matilda, don't worry," he said, "But do you want to know why I came back?"

"I presume it's because you're already falling in love with me," I said teasingly, without thinking.

"Yes, I'm in love," he joked. "No, not yet, at least."

My heart stopped, my breath stuck in my throat. He paused and met my eyes. I handed him the matches, still holding eye contact. He lit the match in one shot and knelt down to light the fire.

"I just wanted you to be okay," he said. "I don't know. I just have this incredible need to care for you."

He looked down, claiming he was crazy. I agreed, but insisted I was too—and had been from the moment I saw him.

Like a perfect gentleman, he didn't stay long in my room; we went back downstairs and stepped outside, since the lobby felt too quiet for our gentle voices. We stayed together, talking for a further thirty minutes, jumping from one topic to another.

Being only one street over from The Seine, I convinced myself that it was colder because of it. I stepped into his warm arms, and he held me against his chest. I clung to his cashmere sweater—a special birthday gift from his dad.

After the divorce, it became difficult for him to spoil his children on an artist's income, but he seemed to always find a way. He preferred to live with the very minimum and give to others.

Yves's sister lived in Paris. As the age gap began to disappear, they became close in adulthood. Being ten years apart, it had been hard to find common interests for a while. Yves had regular contact with his sister and it kept him sane.

I left his arms sadly and dragged my body up to my room. I sat down, alone and quiet, still wrapped in his scarf. He let me keep it for tomorrow. It smelled like him: fresh mandarin, herbs, and various spices. I felt incredible despair and so deeply attached. Already.

I stripped off my clothes and dipped a toe into the shower, my back softly brushing against the towel hanging nearby. I wished it was his touch instead.

That night, it was hard to sleep with so much on my mind. He was enigmatic, charismatic, and kind-hearted. My Yves.

The next day, I jolted out of bed to the blaring sound of someone calling my name. Confused and half-asleep, I stumbled to the window. Not to any surprise, but it was Yves, standing in the street and smiling like an idiot.

"Matilda! *Ma chérie*! Come down!"

His voice echoed through the vacant street, surely waking every sleeping soul, but he didn't seem to care, unapologetically grinning up at me. I couldn't help but laugh at his theatrical display.

I waved him upstairs. I quickly threw on a robe over my satin nightgown, my cheeks flushing at the thought of Yves seeing me so undone. He completely jumped forward four or five dates, but I loved his urgency.

I opened the door and there stood Yves, arms full of pastries, two coffees in 'to-go' cups and a carton of orange juice.

"Good morning," he beamed, stepping inside. "I wasn't sure what you'd like, so I got a bit of everything."

I didn't even realize how many pastries he'd bought on impulse because I was immediately distracted by the matching hotel robe he wore over his clothes. He'd clearly charmed the front desk into giving him one before coming up.

"Matilda, it's 'breakfast in bed.' I had to show up on theme," he said, in complete seriousness. I nodded in agreement, holding back another laugh.

He laid out a spread of buttery croissants, *pain au chocolat*, and *pain suisse* on the small table.

We settled into bed, him lying against the headboard and me, sitting opposite him on the corner. We tore off flaky bits of our croissants and dipped them into creamy cappuccinos.

I couldn't help but think from an outside perspective of the current situation. I was sharing breakfast in bed with a man I'd just met, both of us in hotel robes like we'd known each other for years or most naturally, just spent the night together.

My mind wandered against all restraint. I imagined the sight of his naked body in the morning light and his softly tanned skin against the white cotton duvet.

Our conversation flowed easily, touching on books, dream vacations, and life philosophies.

"I've always wanted to explore the markets in the South of France," I mused, imagining wandering through the tables of antique mirrors, marble ashtrays and gold jewelry.

Yves nodded enthusiastically. "I can't wait to design my house. I want a beautiful garden full of vegetables," he said, hardly taking a breath. "I want to source vintage green tiles for the kitchen and on weekends, a living room full of friends."

As he spoke, his eyes lit up, and I found myself mesmerized. The further he described the house, the more I began to picture myself in it—there, in a lace summer dress, picking tomatoes and parsley from his garden.

"And Yves, imagine there is a dog too. I want a soft dog and we can call her Praline or Cappuccino or something cute like that to match her caramel color," I paused, smiling through my teeth. "And I don't want us to be one of those couples that never allows her on the couch."

He grinned, tight-lipped and puckered as if trying to hold back a smile. I questioned his sudden change in expression.

"Well," he said, laughing. "Do I at least get to choose the color of *our* couch, or have you decided that too?"

My face reddened instantly, my body began to overheat and I felt the overwhelming need to burst into tears of embarrassment. I held it in and apologized.

He did not accept my apology; instead, lifted his body to move across the bed, closer to me. He closed the distance between us and, in one fluid motion, pulled me to his lips. His hand cupped the back of my head, his fingers intertwined in my hair.

The kiss was slow in pace, but sensual in profile. A soft sigh escaped me, quickly swallowed by Yves's mouth. He began to tug at the hem of my robe. I nodded approvingly as he brushed my robe aside just enough to expose my upper thigh. His fingers traced down my leg and gripped my calf, guiding my leg to wrap around his torso. He pulled me into his lap and in a straddle, gently rocked me back and forth. I didn't have to think twice with Yves. It was easy to let myself go, but in a comfortable sense rather than a reckless one.

When our lips parted, Yves rested his forehead against mine. His emerald eyes, raging with desire, searched my face. We agreed to control our impulses and leave the kiss there. For now.

We spent the rest of the morning sipping coffee and sharing stories in our robes; however, Yves had traded the clothes underneath for just the robe. He insisted again that we match, but I was almost certain he only wanted to be nearly naked with me. It felt domestic and comfortable.

As the morning turned to afternoon, we lay in bed, intertwined. I clung to him tightly as clouds departed from the window view. The peaceful silence was often interrupted by the piercing police sirens, but I didn't mind. It only reminded me that the sirens were different than back home and I was truly away.

I traced my finger along his bare skin, the place on the inside of his upper arm—softer than silk. Something rather small to notice, but I did.

He created a gap between his legs for me to sit in. I assumed my place and rested my hands on his thighs. His body tensed up when my touch fell upon him—exactly my intention. "Tell me everything," I whispered with pleading eyes.

"Ask me anything," he replied.

For an hour, we talked, our voices in a low murmur to match the topics at hand. Yves found his voice and recounted his own childhood difficulties. He had often found himself in isolation. Mom and Dad didn't fight discreetly, so when it came time to build relationships, he didn't have much trust in anyone. This went for friends and girlfriends alike.

"I built walls," he admitted. "I learned to protect my happiness. Sometimes, I worry I'm too stubborn about it though."

I reassured him that it was good to be stubborn in certain areas of life. Maybe if I had been more hard-headed in my life, I wouldn't have been internally gutted and robbed of energy in almost every relationship I'd had.

I was someone who grasped the energy of everyone around me and held it close. A family lost on the subway, suitcases dragging behind them and confusion in their voices—I absorbed it all. Their stress was my stress. I couldn't seem to do what the others did—turn a blind eye, remain completely unaffected.

Depression was a persistent character in my life. I didn't spare any details with Yves because I knew he wouldn't play down the matter at hand. And I was right.

"Sometimes, it just feels easier to sink into it. To let the sadness win," I explained, scratching the palm of my hand. "Being happy felt like an enormous task—like a chore I never could stay consistent with."

Yves listened intently. He lifted my hand and pressed a kiss into it. After, he pulled me closer, the warmth of his chest against my cheek. I found it comforting when humans melted into each other like that, hearts synchronized.

I liked Yves. Adored him, actually. Loved him, maybe.

He stood up, loosening the string of his robe. I sat on the edge of the bed, reading him one of my latest poems. I'd never shared them with anyone before. He was left standing before me, in nothing but briefs and his robe thrown next to me. Masculine and towering in height. I knew my fingers were too cold to reach out and touch his chest so I kept them wrapped around my notebook. He took his folded pants from the chair and slipped into them.

He liked to play games with me as much as I liked to toy with him. I didn't finish my poem. He asked me to, but it was impossible with his bare waistline staring me in the face; he stood there, his hand in the pocket of his blue jeans.

He leaned down without a word, just inches from my lips. "Is this the part where you kiss me and tell me you want me?" I said, only partly joking.

"No, but this is the part where I tell you I'm going home," he whispered, "to shower and change before our date tonight.

—

Two knocks at my door exactly two hours later, prompted me to nearly smudge my lipstick—a rosy-brown shade by Chanel. I swung open the door to find Yves behind a bouquet of flowers—a beautiful arrangement of pastel-colored hydrangeas surrounded by baby's breath and greenery. I was someone who liked subtlety over vibrant colors.

Yves sat himself on the bed, waiting for me to finish getting dressed. He was a patient man. I decided on a black satin midi dress that resembled lingerie more than a dress. I threw a wool coat over my shoulders and pulled on black knee-high boots.

The bistro, Yves's choice, was in the seventh arrondissement. *Chez Georges* was designed by Slavik, an architect popular in the '70s. Yves strode in. I was naturally a half-step behind, watching where the sidewalk met the steps. The host's eyes lit up.

"Yves!" He sang. "*Comment vas-tu ?*"

Formal 'vous' abandoned for friendly 'tu.' A language shift, while small to recognize, was large in meaning. The host's gaze flicked to me. Eyebrows rose and a grin, conspiratorial, flashed between them.

Yves's hand was warm on my back. "*Matilda, je te présente Philippe.*"

He smiled a genuine smile; we exchanged cheek kisses—*la bise*—and ended in a kind *Enchantée*.

He led us through the bustle to a table near the bar's clinking glasses and muffled noise from the kitchen. It was a beautifully set table with lit candles and polished silverware. The smoke from the candle danced above our heads.

As if on cue, two glasses of white wine appeared with bread and *foie gras*. Yves smiled that famous smile—the one that wrinkles the sides of his face, eyes to cheeks.

DÉJÀ VU

We took this moment between our *apéritifs* and plates to observe the crowd around us. The richest of the rich and *us*—the sort-of-couple, I thought, falling in love unlike the horribly dull couples portioning off their halves of the cheese course.

We found our focal point, like an artist searching for his next inspiration: a woman across from us. Her lips pursed in disappointment, fixing her gaze on the approaching waiter.

"*Plus de vin*," she commanded, manicured fingers tapping impatiently on the table. The waiter nodded, asking when her husband would arrive.

The wooden floors creaked as he arrived dressed in a heavy overcoat. Fashionably late. He carefully draped his coat over the back of his chair, purposely exposing the Hermès tag.

"*Pardon ma chérie, le métro*," he offered with a Gallic shrug before sliding into his seat. His apology was met with an eye-roll and exhausted sigh.

Enough money for Hermès, but took the *métro*. Perhaps it was a coat from his father, or perhaps, against all direct assumptions, he was rather rich but chose the *métro* merely to keep himself humble and connected to the people. Must be the old money thing.

The woman leaned across the table, her pearls brushing the white tablecloth. A ripple of laughter, carefully pitched, radiated through the room, but never left the table. Paris lived in that laughter—elegant, knowing, ever so slightly wicked.

Our plates arrived with a *"bon appétit"* and placed so delicately in front of us. Yves's plate of escargot arrived swimming in garlic and parsley. I ordered a plate of Coquilles Saint-Jacques—buttery and light.

Our dessert, an *Île Flottante*, arrived in a bowl bigger than our heads. Yves explained that it was made with vanilla from Madagascar and *crème anglaise*—a dessert Americans weren't typically familiar with.

Midnight struck and Yves dragged me into a bar nearby. The quiet bar upstairs turned into a chaotic nightclub downstairs; Yves told me that a place like this reflected my personality—that I might seem like one thing, but I would always find a way to be another.

Yves nodded to the barman and pulled me down a narrow set of stairs. Either he was known here or simply had a face that allowed him everywhere on the account that he was beautiful. The music was loud and '80s. We danced, throwing our heads and hair around. Reminded me of my teenage years in the city. Raging teenager then, carefully-calculated adult now.

On the cab ride back to my hotel, my hand found his upper thigh in-between tipsy laughs. His body tightened. Somehow, it felt like I'd been here before. In this very moment of ecstasy and temptation: back of a cab, loose lips, *déjà vu*.

5

June

Tipsy and falling out of the cab, we managed to make our way into the lobby of The Hotel Chelsea. It was quiet, yet packed with people hanging on the walls and lounging on couches. Funnily enough, The Rolling Stones were on the record player. Halos of smoke hung around people's heads. Every ashtray overflowed. Haziness hung in their eyes and cigarettes from their mouths.

Claude was attached at my hip, following the stairs to his room. He struggled to find the key in his pocket.

In his room, the door slammed shut between kisses as we abandoned our clothes, leaving a trail of garments across the floor before he melted into my lips.

We were struck by the cold air blowing in from the window. It was left open all night; I jumped into bed and covered myself under the duvet. Claude raced to close the window and pull the curtain. Caught in a loop of laughter,

Claude, completely nude in the brightness of our room, accidentally flashed our neighbors in the darkness of night. We laughed about it and dimmed the bedside lamps.

He settled into bed and wedged himself into the curves of my body. The hairs on my neck came alive under the touch of his tongue. Goosebumps. Everywhere, they traveled behind my ear directly to the hairs standing up on my scalp.

I filled his eardrums with soft moans as his fingers danced inside me. He was generous and yet still, a disciplined dancer. He danced on *relevé* and managed perfectly timed *fouetté* turns and elegant leaps across my stage. I managed to point my toes throughout this duo.

Chest to chest, I pulled him inside me. Warmth filled my body. Sweat dripped from his forehead, falling between my breasts. His hands were everywhere, leaving trails of fire on my skin.

This was where I belonged, in this moment, with him. This could have been a battle between mind and heart, but it wasn't. I wanted to dive in headfirst—this wasn't a distraction or a mindless fling.

We dragged ourselves out of bed and into the shower. He was a beautiful man, his body soft yet carved. He quickly turned into an improv dancer, returning to the stage for an *encore*. We used all the hot water that night—our neighbors were pissed the next morning.

Afterwards, we lay tangled together; Claude pressed a kiss to my forehead as I drifted off. I felt him watch me for a few minutes before he too lost consciousness and surrendered to his pillow.

I didn't mind being barefaced and undone in his arms.

6

Matilda

The next morning, we were woken by the sun pouring in. Yves lay beside me, his breathing still deep and even. I slipped out of bed, a bit sore from last night, and wrapped myself in a robe before ordering room service in hesitant French.

Cold tile greeted my feet as I stepped into the bathroom; I faced the mirror, and a stranger stared back—confident and changed. My fingers wove through my hair, finding echoes of last night—a soft tangle here, a whisper of a kiss there.

I traced invisible outlines on my neck where his lips had been. He had been soft yet insistent with me; the ghost of his touch danced along my skin.

It was a night of firsts and spontaneity, but somehow felt familiar, like we had rehearsed it before. Dancers in another lifetime.

I assumed my usual spot in front of the window while Yves turned in bed. I waited for a tap at the door, gazing down at the street, alive with the commotion of midday truck deliveries.

A beautiful spread arrived at our doorstep. Yves stirred in bed. Hard to say whether it was the knock at the door, or the smell of coffee that woke him.

We settled into bed, picking at our plates and falling into a comfortable silence. Eventually, Yves spoke.

"So, Matilda," he paused, "and don't take it the wrong way."

I gulped, afraid he was going to tell me he was going to leave. "Can I help you pay for the room service?" he blurted out.

"You're staying in Paris for two weeks. It costs a fortune as a tourist. Even as locals, we can't afford much two weeks after payday."

I softly smiled. I'd just realized that I didn't really say anything about my parents' professional lives. "Let me explain, but don't change your opinion about me," I said. "I know you won't, but-"

Yves raised an eyebrow.

"My dad, in the early '80s, struck luck as a lawyer in the city. Big cases. One of the highest paying jobs at that time and still is," I said. "He works constantly. I don't see much of him."

Yves was endearing in the way he listened. Like he was listening to a bird sing its song—caught in a trance with eyes wide and ears open.

I continued, "My mom stayed home so I could have at least one constant parent in my life. She was tough, but present. Wasn't an open book by any means, but there."

I gulped, my mouth dry, "As for money, it was important to my parents that I went to public school and didn't lose touch with normalcy. My parents have money; however, we don't scream about it. I wanted to use my savings for this trip, but with a father as a lawyer, you don't win arguments very often."

He preferred that I save my money for my future, saying I would need it to fund my own fashion line. I told him numerous times that I didn't want to be a fashion designer—he always seemed to listen with just one ear.

Reassuring me, he said, "Matilda, don't be scared to tell me things."

I hesitated, "Money divides people. I didn't want it to change anything."

At that time, money was seemingly a forbidden conversation topic. Like age, for some. With Yves though, it wasn't something worth avoiding.

We danced around relationship labels; considering we only knew each other for one week, these conversations felt like blueprints—the base for our future.

He asked questions, I answered. It was nice to have an equal sided relationship. There was no need to justify my background. I was simply Matilda—no more, no less.

Yves adjusted in bed, sipping his coffee. He shot me a smile looking through his eyebrows.

"You said something about a fashion line," he said. "You work in fashion?"

"I study Fashion Design at Parsons and work at my friend's coffee shop in Greenwich Village when I can. It's called The Fox."

His ears seemed to perk up. "I'd like to see it sometime," he said.

I nodded. "You'll love it. It used to be a hub for cool people in the late '60s. The stage was removed, but the bar was kept."

Yves struggled to find his words. "I just-" he said, "The name sounds familiar. Must have read it somewhere—maybe in a book about New York I borrowed once from the library."

A moment of silence passed between us.

"So, you study Fashion Design," he said, shaking the feeling off. "*C'est incroyable*."

I blushed red. Yves made me feel supported, like I was doing something monumental.

"I am, yes," I said. "It's mainly for understanding the field, creating a couple things, but what really interests me is textiles."

I ran my fingers along the edge of the tablecloth, feeling its grainy texture. "I want to be a buyer—controlling quality, working with the production team, balancing the creative with the budget..."

My voice started to jump in octaves and excitement. "I want to work for houses like Hermès or Dior," I said. "Not just for the glamour, but for the challenge."

I paused, considering my words. "It's a luxury to love clothes you wear, and that starts with what they're made of. I want to be the person who takes care of that."

His gaze was encouraging—the type of look that propels you to accomplish your goals. And there it was. That big smile that wrinkled his eyes down to his cheeks. We finished our *petit-déjeuner* and made love after.

—

The following week was my last one. When Yves wasn't working, we were together and covered lots of ground in Paris.

We visited Monet's water lilies; we bounced from Café de Flore to Les Deux Magots pretending to be intellectual poets. Feeling quite inspired by Yves and the city, I wrote a few unfinished poems that I would never revisit; they existed as they were, and I wouldn't do anything to change that. We danced in clubs until four o'clock in the morning with his friends.

I saw his apartment. He lived in the eleventh arrondissement. A classic Parisian apartment built in the early 1900s with original door handles and moldings. He kept his apartment illuminated with various lamps he found at vintage markets, casting orange and warm lighting. Every color, texture, pattern was thoughtfully coordinated.

That week, I dragged him into a pizzeria. We took a slice each and ate directly from the plate like New Yorkers—his turn for a cultural education.

"*Chez moi*, we do like this," I said. "*Dans la rue*."

I was becoming fluent in *franglais* after just two weeks with Yves; we couldn't commit to one language per conversation because there are words the English language can't express like French does—'*Ce n'est pas grave*' being one of them.

I took that one home with me and used it in times of distress. It had more depth than repeating "It's okay, it's okay" to myself. "*Grave*" was more complex. In English, we use this word; "You are in grave danger." Not to be confused with a "grave," or "tombstone," however.

I was raised to feel and express myself in English, yet it was a foreign language that comforted me the most in times of trouble.

I tried to cling onto every word. He and his friends advanced my high school level French and replaced it with the real language. Implementing slang and dropping grammar rules to speak faster with your friends.

After only two weeks, French culture had followed me home. It was integrated in my DNA in a way I couldn't explain.

—

Our last week in Paris had a serenity to it—romantic and thoughtful. Fearing time was moving too fast, we made love everyday, hoping to slow the seconds we had left.

He was soul-stirring. My muse. My heart's echo.

And I didn't want to leave him.

My Yves.

7

June

We held hands, dragging his luggage behind with the other. JFK Airport. The inevitable was finally upon us: Claude was leaving New York.

I was distraught. Unable to find my words, I replaced them with soft cries, clinging to his arm like a sloth hanging by the branches.

We listened to the radio, in hopes of distracting our wandering minds. It was October 25, 1964, and The Stones were meant to play *The Ed Sullivan Show* that night. They were starting to be all rage in the states. "Time Is On My Side" jumped the charts after their appearance. And I had danced with Mick a few nights before- a crazy night, the kind you tell your kids about one day.

The airport air felt dense and lifeless, at least to me. I stood frozen at the check-in counter with Claude while he rummaged through his bag for his passport. He had a beautiful messenger style bag. It was a worn brown color and lay against his body perfectly. It was nice to see a man so well-suited in his style.

Above, the clicking split-flap board startled me out of empty disassociation.

Flip. Paris. Flip. London. Flip. Rome.

Each click caused my body to flinch and overstimulate, like a pulsing heartbeat of departures and arrivals. My eyes were sweating with anxiety.

Claude's hand rested on my back—warm, but useless against the numbness I felt inside.

We sat side by side, our hands intertwined, waiting for the final boarding call. The airport operated around us—flight attendants scanning passes, pilots huddled around the gate sipping their last drops of coffee—but we existed in our own bubble.

It was a hazy place, dark, anticipating a thunderstorm. The world held its breath as distant rumbles shook the ground we stood on. Our brittle bodies, decayed by melancholy, awaited the storm's destruction. And so, we sat motionless, caught in a world of the inescapable.

"Once a month," Claude said, breaking the silence. "We can plan a phone call once a month."

I nodded, my throat tight. International calls were steep in price and poor in connection. The calls were often noisy and required an overseas operator who would connect you to the inward operator in that country. At nearly $11 per minute, we could only manage a few. A hundred dollars a week was considered good pay, so as struggling artists in music, we stayed realistic.

I couldn't call from my parents' house either. My dad made several international calls but his assistant logged every call he ever made. They would be suspicious not only of the cost each month but also of why their daughter was regularly calling France. It was a lost cause so I opted to pay Margot the extra charges each month.

"I don't know how to do this," I whispered, my voice cracking. "How to say goodbye."

Claude traced circles on my hand. "Then let's not say goodbye. Say you will come visit me in Paris."

I looked up at him, falling into the soft curve of his smile, the depth in his eyes. "Until next time," I uttered, the words tasting bittersweet on my tongue.

I loved him. It was irrational, maybe even foolish, but undeniably true. I had fallen in love with him in mere hours.

The PA system crackled in static, announcing the final call. We hesitantly stood, still holding hands, neither wanting to be the first to move.

"June," he said, his voice low and urgent. "I'm in love with you."

I held my breath, wondering if he had read my mind.

He continued, "I'm sorry to tell you this now, but I couldn't tell you in a letter or with a shitty phone connection. I-"

"Claude," I interrupted. "I- I love you too."

Tears filled my waterline and flooded onto my cheeks; I let out a big breath, smiling through my teeth. I reached to cup Claude's face in my hands. His slight stubble scratched against my palms.

Claude's eyes started to glass over before pulling my body flush against his. He was urgent and fairly gentle. We kissed. Passionately and without ending. Until it did.

Saying our final goodbye was like a slow car crash: you see it coming and yet, you can't do anything to stop it. You struggle with the wheel, the tires squeal against asphalt, the car inching toward you—it's all in view, as if in slow motion. And then the crash, the tragedy of goodbyes and the unimaginable pain after—twist of the knife to the heart, the mending of metal.

As Claude walked away, disappearing into the crowd, a piece of my soul went with him. I stood there watching long after he'd vanished from sight, already spiraling into panic.

I wanted to run after him. I played out the entire cinematic scene: pushing everyone through the crowd, yelling his name. I wanted him to deboard the plane because he loved me; we'd kiss, and everyone waiting at the nearby gate would applaud.

I quickly snapped out of my daydream and looked up to the flight board. Paris: ALL ABOARD. I turned my back on it and sat down, dissolving into desperate cries. I steadied myself, hands pressed to my knees as tears fell from my eyes, landing in small, individual droplets on my jeans; I held my heart, afraid it would fall out.

I wasn't the kind of girl to cry for a man, but I'd fallen in love. He wasn't my only source of happiness, but I wouldn't mind waking up to his company every morning either.

I could hear Margot's voice echo: "Be his midnight muse and leave 'em in the dust." And I did just that. Before Claude.

When he entered The Fox, all the particles in my body defrosted from their prior state of perpetual winter, where I'd kept my heart frozen—safe from becoming another casualty of male deception.

I threw myself headfirst into my music career after Claude left. I began playing better shows to bigger crowds. My setlist had grown to fifteen songs and the band and I became super close. Margot loved to see Rob and I picking at each other.

She would say, "You two are the loves of my life," pulling us into a huddled hug. "I never was good at decision-making, so you guys are both stuck with me."

Margot and I grew to be like sisters; she held me in the times I missed Claude and helped me translate my messy words in well-written letters. She continued her quest in making me bilingual too. She encouraged full days of speaking strictly in French. She kept my mind occupied and orderly.

My set was eventually seen by Manny Roth, the owner/manager of *Cafe Wha?* He called my style "poetically sexy." I was reaching people.

To my surprise, he invited me to play on a Friday night; he had high hopes and wanted to simulate a true trial run. The crowd's reaction would be the "tell-all" as to whether I would be invited back as a regular. I had finally struck luck after years of sneaking out of my parents' house and lying about my whereabouts.

That night, I ran to the phone at Margot's apartment. Claude and I had a phone call planned in three days, but I couldn't wait. The operator patched me through. I waited, leaning against the wall.

I fidgeted, bursting with excitement similar to a sugar-intoxicated child. Margot stood beside me, dragging out the last moments of a cigarette between her lips. She smoked to the very end, fire nearly burning her fingers every time. Margot hated to waste.

The line crackled and I found a happily confused Claude on the other line. The countdown started: 3 minutes on the clock.

Claude: "What day is it? What happened?"

June: "I'm playing a gig at *Cafe Wha?* this Friday."

The line went silent.

June: "Claude, I can't see your reaction, you know!"

Claude: "Sorry, I'm just speechless. And so proud of you! I knew you would land something big soon."

June: "You always believed in me."

I blushed, turning red in color. Margot shoved me and pulled the phone from my grasp.

Margot: "*Claude, ce n'est pas juste!* I don't get the same reaction when I tell her that."

We laughed. I missed being all together at the bar, drunk and sharing entertaining anecdotes for hours, speaking fluent nonsense.

I ripped the phone from her hand. Claude and I talked quickly through topics.

2 minutes, 15 seconds left.

June: "How are you? How's your work project going?"

Claude: "Good, working a lot. Keeping myself busy. I may have a big tour deal coming in soon. Big band. British and all the rage. We will see what happens, but maybe it could mean traveling back to New York. *Mais comment ça va, ma chérie?*"

1 minute, 45 seconds left.

June: "I want to hear more about this band, write it to me. I'm great, just deciding my set list. I think I will end with the new one, "Boy in Blue." And Sonny, from The Fox, agreed to stay open later tomorrow night so I can try it out with the band."

1 minute left.

Claude: "I miss you. It's only been two weeks. I still can't sleep well."

June: "I do too. I see you everywhere I go. I see your face in strangers. When I close my eyes too."

45 seconds left.

June: "We will make it through this. Let me get through school, make my parents happy. And maybe, you can move to New York because of this new band deal."

Claude: "It's not confirmed. Nothing is set in stone. I don't know how long we will have to wait like this, counting our minutes and the weeks for a letter to arrive in the mail."

He paused.

30 seconds left. And a shift in mood.

Claude: "Everything feels so spontaneous at this age, especially this gig. It's like we need to let the opportunities find us and decide our paths."

June: "But I want to be with you. Now."

15 seconds left.

Claude: "Me too. You're all I think about and write about, talk about. Let's stay positive and focused; our lives are meant to link together—I just know it. We will find luck in New York. Believe in your city."

June: "I know you're right. Take care of yourself and good luck for your tour deal."

Claude: "I love you. And good luck for your show. You will kill it, and I want to hear about it next month."

We laughed. Definitely not a joyous one, more painful than anything else.

Claude: "Bye, sweetie."

June: "Bye."

The line disconnected, leaving me in the emptiness of a phone call with no one on the other side—like space itself, cold and infinitely dark.

That week, I found myself in a depressive state, but it transformed into creativity and inspired intellect. I had lyrics scribbled onto practically every surface: takeout napkins, my hand, nearby mail envelopes. If an idea had come to me, I think I would have been insane enough to write it on the walls in marker.

I was singing constantly, wanting my new song to feel like muscle memory by the time I performed it. A few adjustments were made to the melody that week. I felt good, secure in myself.

It was November 1964, a Friday night at *Cafe Wha?*, and I stepped onto the dimly lit stage. Fifteen songs. The crowd, a sea of unfamiliar faces, watched me closely. My voice rang out, clear and strong. I sang of love and loss, of friendship, of change. The audience swayed, raised their glasses and chanted out.

After my set, I hovered near the bar with Margot, partly because I needed a celebratory drink and partly to delay hearing Manny's decision, avoiding him completely.

I sported my signature look that night: hair artfully disheveled, Bardot eyeliner, heeled boots and my fur jacket. I looked tortured, fatigued by loss, yet still baby-faced.

I lost myself in thought. I craved him—his voice crawling up my neck, hands up my back; I longed for that electricity again.

Suddenly, hands gripped my waist and spun me around. Reminded me of when Claude spun my chair around when we first met. Pure shock jolted through me. It couldn't be him. A stranger's face greeted me—all confidence yet little to no substance behind those eyes.

"What are you drinking?" he asked.

I shot back, eyebrow raised, "Why do you want to know?"

He looked flabbergasted. "Because I want to buy you one."

"What for?" I challenged.

He shrugged, almost shyly. He continued, "It's something you do before-"

I cut him off with a smirk.

"I'm totally trying to freak you out. I'd love a drink, but there's no 'after' to that 'before' you were talking about. I'm already with someone."

"Fair enough," he conceded. "Where is this guy?"

"Not here," I replied, melancholy creeping into my voice.

His brow furrowed. "How can he leave someone sexy like you all alone?"

He disgusted me. He sought validation in a way that only questioned his relationship with women and why, in reality, they scared him.

I said nothing following his question because it wasn't that simple. He *had* to go back home to his life, follow his career. He'd chosen that path before me. I couldn't expect him to change the course of his life, no matter how sure we were. Even people like us, tempted by excitement, creating art and telling stories, needed to set limits.

I loved him. He loved me. But nothing is ever that simple.

The weight of unspoken words hung between this stranger and I. The bar's chatter increased and swarmed in around us. My blood boiled in agitation. I was flustered, reaching my breaking point, like a boiling kettle squealing on the stovetop.

"I gotta get out of here. Don't follow me," I said, my words sharp as a knife.

Manny caught me in my race down the tables. "Kid," he said, "you've got something special." He offered me a regular spot. My world shifted at that moment. I had found my stage in the place where recognition is promised.

I left the bar that night with the bittersweetness of good news on my tongue. I had my dream venue, but not my dream guy. I almost didn't want Manny to catch me leaving. Or I wanted him to hate the set, tell me to get lost, say I had no talent —and then I'd fall into the arms of Claude in Paris. I'd work a little job and sing in shitty jazz clubs to anyone who understood English.

I was completely irrational and ridiculous. But it was just a fleeting thought, because I was playing at *Cafe Wha?* and completely over the moon about it. Finally, I had *that* moment— the one where everything feels like it could happen for you.

But like all moments of serenity and hopefulness, reality hits you in the face during the early hours after sleepless nights; I was becoming a sort of insomniac, depressive at these hours.

The time it took to wait for a letter made me feel like I was going crazy. I jotted down all the noteworthy things that happened during the day, but I was writing to no one. At that moment in time, I wanted to share the funny anecdote and have it be a memory after. After two to three weeks of waiting for a reaction to a simple story, it was no longer something memorable; the moment had passed.

I wrote a letter. I played my gigs. I received his letter.

I called him for three minutes. I played my gigs. I sent another letter.

Our lives revolved around that same cycle for one year.

Meanwhile, I perfected my gigs at *Cafe Wha?*, grew bilingual in French thanks to Margot, and wrote close to thirty songs.

Claude, unfortunately, didn't get that touring job in New York like we'd hoped for. He stayed in Paris; he couldn't risk starting over in a new city with opportunities so close like that. I was worried he would fall into a depression due to months of zero luck, but it wasn't in Claude's character to throw in the towel.

I wrote and waited for his response. I waited nearly two months.

AUDRIANA CRISTELLO

To my lovely June,

I apologize for the wait, ma chérie. Tu me manques énormément. How can I live without your laugh? How can I wake up another day without you?

Yesterday, on the metro, I saw a woman who looked just like you. My heart collapsed. I must have scared her based on my reaction. I felt inclined to tell her about you. I keep the picture you sent in my wallet. I showed the woman. She said "Elle me ressemble quand j'étais jeune." I wasn't completely crazy.

I may have found an opportunity here in Paris. It's a French band. A bit at the end of their run. I feel like after this tour, they will break up. They all like each other, just losing passion for their work. It's something to do for now. But I can understand their frustration. I hope something great comes along soon.

How are you, June? I wish I could see you play at The Wha. Have you changed up your look for shows? Or is my sweet June still wearing her famous fur like the day I met her?

Going forward we should include a photograph in every letter we send. I want more photos from you dear. To see you each month will give me strength.

Short letter this time, not much of an update for you this month. I love you.

Pour toujours. xo
Your Claude

I held his letter against my chest, like you would a teddy bear. I held back tears as my nose stung and my ears closed up.

He didn't forget about me. The truth was, I could have sent another letter during his silence, but I didn't have the energy. In reality, dragging myself to the mailbox felt like a walk of shame.

Still, he wrote so well. As time continued, I found his writing increasingly more poetic. We experienced, we shared, but strictly in writing. I wanted to share a moment in real time and together, not independently.

And so, I wept because although we share the same sky, when the morning sun shone down on Paris, the moon still lingered in Manhattan's shadow.

8

Matilda

I wept because all I had left of Yves was his home address and phone number scribbled onto a piece of paper. It was quite an eerie moment, watching him write it all down. The pain felt familiar, which oddly comforted me.

I had a few photos of us, together: one along the Seine, taken by a sweet older couple, another of us dressed up for that dinner at *Chez Georges*. Otherwise, I had collected independent photos of Yves—serving breakfast, posing in front of statues, wearing a beret outside a souvenir shop.

I brushed my hair, staring back at myself in the mirror. Pristinely clean mirror, like I had left it weeks ago. Only, the woman in the reflection had changed; she had been found and now lost. I had left here heartbroken by one, and now I returned devastated by another.

With each strand of hair I brushed, Yves's scent mingled and conversed with the air that surrounded me. Herbs, citrus and spices. My Yves.

It brought me back to our first night together. He had felt so strong and confident in the way he held me. I stared off, my eyes glazing over, remembering every moment so clearly: my hotel room was calm and warmed by the fire, the sheets were freshly washed and felt like clouds.

I could have sworn I felt his fingertips crawling up my back. My mouth lacked saliva, but I tried to roll it down anyway. I remembered the way his lips crawled up my arm; my breath caught in my throat. I wished this hallucination was real. Nonetheless, I stood there, eyes flickering with imagination behind them. I gripped the countertop as his voice warmed my ear.

When he touched me it was too surreal to understand. He was magnetic, rare, like someone you'd never met before, yet somehow you knew you had.

—

It was December of 1994, soon New Year. I liked the beginning of months. Always felt like a fresh start, like you were given this new strength and confidence to begin again.

It was 80 cents per ounce for an international letter that year. It took about two to three weeks for our letters to be delivered. The price seemed to advance, but the shipping time hadn't budged for decades.

I hoped I wouldn't be in a long-distance relationship long enough to complain about the price jump each year.

Writing letters to each other felt ridiculous for the time because three years prior, AOL email was introduced in the United States. It was the birth of a new age for communication. It felt like a hopeful time, but for us, quite bittersweet. Europe was not yet on AOL.

I checked my mailbox religiously those first few weeks. Each day harbored the same loneliness, the same echo of metal closing on nothing addressed to me. When his first letter arrived, my hands trembled as I carried it upstairs. I was very aware then that he had touched that letter. If it hadn't been so unsanitary, I would have kissed it just to feel close to him again.

The words he wrote made poetry seem pale. He wrote of Paris in winter, how the gray sky mimicked his days without me. He caught himself often turning to share history anecdotes about the city with someone who wasn't there. My throat ached reading it.

I wrote back immediately with my initial feelings, ink flowing like confession. I wrote about the phantom conversations I had with him on the subway too, how catching a whiff of sandalwood on a customer at work would make my heart stop. From the outside, I must have looked insane to everyone on the subway—a woman caught accidentally talking to herself—but truthfully, I was doing okay.

I had to look at the bigger picture, a more positive one. Nonetheless, I was lucky to have Yves in my life; I was fortunate to study something I loved and happy to work with my friend in a quiet coffee shop. And we were only growing closer with age.

Lola and I found each other on the subway. I hopped on the train, running late to class, and my book had fallen out from under my arm. I had forgotten a bag big enough to throw it into. Lola, a stranger at the time, who was heading for the same train, picked it up and nearly got crushed by the closing doors. She handed me the book and I thanked her ten times.

We briefly talked about what we were doing in life and exchanged phone numbers before I ran to class. We met up later that week at The Fox. I started working there very soon after.

—

I started marking up my calendar—sent letter, received letter, sent letter—like the assistant of a punctual lawyer. It was quite possible I'd leaped at the opportunity to organize like this because I had seen my father's assistant doing the same when I was younger.

Three weeks felt like forever when your heart was at the mercy of the postal service.

Some nights were harder than others; I'd lie awake, reminiscing about how he'd trace shapes on my skin. The memory was so vivid it hurt: our faces so close, the way he'd murmur "*mon cœur*" against my temple.

On restless nights like that, I'd throw my body out of bed and write him pages of everything I couldn't remember in the light of day. I wrote a lot in those first few months.

Ever since I left him, I felt like I was suffocating in every room of the house. The only air that felt relieving was the air outside—maybe because the air was fresh, crisper and natural, but truly it was because I liked to imagine the breeze blowing against my rosy cheeks had graced his face too.

Having his words but not his touch was the hardest part to cope with. The words "*tu me manques*" felt hollow on paper, nothing like when he'd whisper them against my skin. I threw myself into work and school to distract my wandering mind. I wanted to stay positive; I knew we would be together. One day.

I delve into my thoughts late at night though—the exquisite pain of separation, the way distance makes the heart grow not just fonder, but deeper. In my more poetic moments, I imagined our letters crossing over the Atlantic, our carefully chosen words soon to be read and whispered aloud by the other. In my darker moments, I wondered if this would be enough for him, just until I graduated.

We had discussed our future while together in Paris. The thought came to us naturally, as if it were already decided for us. Just required some patience to what felt like fate.

—

It was June of 1995, my birthday month. I invited Lola and a couple friends from school for my birthday dinner at an Italian restaurant in Greenwich Village. I didn't have many friends, but I preferred it that way. It was rare for me to have genuine connections with people. I couldn't stand the friendships where you talked just for the sake of talking.

Lola and I worked together until late afternoon. It was a busy Saturday, and we barely had time to rest. After the closure, we ramped up the volume on the radio and changed into our outfits. We loved getting ready to the 80s station; Soft Cell's "Tainted Love" was my song. I wore a dress I'd made at school. It was made of silk with cut-outs of lace that made it playful and sexy, but not vulgar. I liked this new version of myself—the Matilda I aspired to be: confident, well-read and creatively stimulated.

We were cocktail-drunk before our plates arrived. The staff, who were our age and incredibly fun, banged on pots and pans and danced on the chairs with us. I fell down into the booth when our plates appeared. I had truffle pasta with a cocktail on the way. I requested a song, again "Tainted Love," and sang off-key. The tiramisu was incredible. One of my favorite desserts.

My birthday was nearly perfect—just missed one person in attendance.

—

The halls of Parsons became my sanctuary. I spent hours in the textile lab, fingers running over fabrics, learning their feel. Each material has their own set of rules and it is necessary to understand them before asking a fabric to bend and form into what you want.

My first real piece was the slip dress I made for my birthday. It made me think of moonlight in Paris. I worked on it late into the night, when the studio was empty and I could enjoy the stress-free environment. I'd chosen merlot-colored silk. It fell to the floor like spilled water, held up by the thinnest of straps. I used the most delicate lace for cutouts around the torso —resembling intricate spider webs. I thought of Yves as I hand-stitched the lace trim, wondering if he would appreciate it.

Lola took a polaroid of me in the dress that night, smiling behind a glass of wine. I sent it to Yves, along with my latest letter.

—

I received his letter just as July began. His handwriting looked rushed, excited even. As I read, my heart seemed to stop and restart with each word.

He was coming to New York. December 1995. Three weeks that would stretch into January—Christmas, New Year's, all of it together. I read the letter four times, his words blurring through my tears. Over a year had passed since we last touched, since I'd heard his voice outside of memory and dreams.

The paper held his excitement: he'd found a cheaper flight, arranged time off work, and already dreamed up places we would go—The Met, Central Park in the snow, my little apartment that he knew only through my descriptions.

My body hummed with anticipation. Those ten months felt both endless and fleeting. I would see my Yves again. Touch his face, hear his laugh, watch his eyes crinkle when he smiles.

9

June

The letters became sparser after that first year. What started as weekly correspondence dwindled to monthly, then to every few months. We talked about visiting each other—always talked about it—but something would come up: a big show for me, an important advancement for him in work.

Our last exchange had been two months ago; I kept the letter in my bedside drawer, reading it so many times the paper had gone soft at the creases. Claude was making it big in Paris with an underground band called Les Sauvages. They played this raw, gritty rock that was taking over the bar scene. He managed them brilliantly, turning dive-bar gigs into sold-out venues, pulling younger crowds.

Meanwhile, I was living my dream. Show after show, my voice grew stronger and my audience larger. I was exhausted, but electric with it. Some nights I'd stumble home at 3 A.M.

Margot would joke that I was becoming a proper rock star. At that time, I traded my fur coat for leather.

But in those quiet moments before sleep, when the city's pulse slowed to a murmur, I'd think of Claude, wondering if he still ached for me, if he still loved me.

I lay there, convincing myself our passion hadn't died—it had just been buried under the weight of our separate lives, different time zones, our growing success. One day it would fall into place. Somehow.

His last letter mentioned a possible American tour for Les Sauvages. "Maybe then," he wrote, "we can finally cross this ocean between us." But I'd learned not to hold my breath; we were both changing, growing into versions of ourselves we'd only dreamed of being.

Still, every time I took the stage, I'd scan the crowd. Just in case. Just maybe. But I was always greeted by his ghost in the back booth and the echoing rattle of his boots across the floor.

I kept singing, and Paris kept its hold on him. We were moving forward, even if it meant moving apart.

10

Matilda

Terminal 4 at JFK buzzed with December's chaos: a father counted off the luggage still missing while the mother breastfed one child and tried to round up the other two from running around the baggage claim. Complete chaos.

I paced the arrivals hall, my heels clicking against the worn tile floor. The air was thick with anticipation and the smell of exhaust fumes pushing hard from the cars outside the doors. My heart raced with each new wave of passengers.

Then I saw him.

Yves emerged through the sliding doors, his dark hair tousled from the long flight. He wore the same camel coat from our days in Paris, now wrinkled from being balled up and used as a pillow for nine hours. Our eyes met across the crowded hall, and suddenly, every molecule in my body seemed to assume their right places. As if I had been struggling with some kind of rare *maladie* before and upon sight, he suggested all the cells in my body regenerate instantaneously.

He dropped his bags.

"*Ma chérie*," he breathed into my hair, his voice sending electricity down my spine. He smelled like the artificial air conditioning on planes and that distinctive mix of citrus and oud that was uniquely him. I pressed my face into his neck, inhaling deeply.

The cab ride home was a blur of comfortable silence and timid glances. It was a ridiculous feeling—feeling shy, even though I'd already seen this person naked in the intimate morning light.

Snow fell outside the window, coating the city in a gentle white blanket. Yves watched in wonder as we crossed into Manhattan territory.

"It's exactly how you described it," he whispered, squeezing my hand. I loved to see him happy.

My apartment felt different with him in it—warmer, fuller. He stood in my tiny living room, taking in the space he had only known through letters. The radiator hissed softly in the corner, fighting against the December chill.

"Show me everything," he said, pulling me close. "Every corner you've written about."

I led him through my world: the windowsill where I drank my morning coffee, the desk where I wrote my letters to him, the nightstand where I kept every letter he had written over the past year.

That first night, we barely slept. We lay tangled in my sheets, our bodies remembering each other; the streetlight filtered through my curtains, casting shadows across his naked skin. His hands found the familiar curves of my body, each touch like *déjà vu* from our nights before.

"I missed this little mark here," he murmured, kissing the scar along the inside of my arm—a bee sting that I picked at relentlessly as a child. It never quite healed.

His hands danced along my rib cage. I squirmed under his fingertips. "And how your breath catches when I touch you here," he said.

We talked until dawn, filling in the gaps that letters couldn't express. He told me about the chaos of his latest project, restoring a jazz club in Montmartre while I shared stories about my design classes, about the clothing I made and the connections I was creating.

"Show me what you're working on," he said, propping himself up on an elbow. The duvet lying against his torso, his chest exposed and inviting.

I slipped out of bed, pulling on his sweater for warmth, and retrieved my sketchbook. I sat cross-legged on the bed, his chin resting on my knee as I flipped through the pages. I showed him the lace dress I had designed; reaching across the bed for the armchair, I pulled the dress into reach. He held the silk as if it might fall through his fingertips. He was gentle and respectful.

"Try it on," he said. "Please."

There was sincerity in the way he begged. It was sexy.

I stood tall. He lay at the foot of the bed, head lingering between my legs. I slipped off his sweater and stepped into the dress I had created upon request. He sat up, on his knees now, possessing my body, his hands finding their way up my legs. His face was always so warm.

He asked me to put on clothes just so he could take them off again.

—

The days that followed were a beautiful blur. We explored the city together, seeing it through each other's eyes.

At the Met, Yves would stop in front of a sculpture, explaining its history, and other visitors would gather around to listen, assuming he was a tour guide. He had borrowed a book from his neighborhood library about the history of New York a while back and had a freakish memory for things like this.

In Central Park, we ice-skated; I fell five times and Yves, never. I was frustrated. At that time, it was Yves who helped me dig into what he called, *mes défauts*. I hated making mistakes—so much so that if I did, I wrestled myself to death trying to fix what had already been done. Impossible. And I was impossibly tired. I never could let myself live it down either. My mind would replay the moment continuously until sadness ultimately flooded my cheeks.

I cried in the arms of Yves, convinced I had a brain far beyond a simple fix. I needed a complete rewiring, an overhaul.

He held me and said, "It's okay to cry, you know. Even if it seems wrong or silly, cry."

He never pushed my feelings down. Instead, he comforted me on an icy bench, in Central Park, amongst the chaos of ice skaters in thirty-degree weather. I was seen and understood. I could cry. Ugly cry, if I wanted.

"Sometimes," I mumbled, wiping my tears. "Sometimes, I worry that it's going to be too much to handle. I'm not happy and optimistic every day, and oftentimes, I don't necessarily have a reason; I feel everything too deeply."

He chuckled softly to himself, "Most great writers and designers do; they find beauty and pain within anything."

I laughed. I did emote with intensity. It takes over my entire nervous system. But after, I could string along a set of words and have it read like poetry.

"Listen," he said, resting his forehead against mine. "I'd rather a woman who feels too much than nearly nothing at all." He smiled that famous eye-crinkling smile.

"It's not a weakness. So cry, feel, be sad. This is the true human experience," he said. "Just means you're alive."

He gently nudged me back out onto the ice and I skated with his help. I was truly a horrible skater, and that was okay.

DÉJÀ VU

—

On a crisp morning, I brought Yves to The Fox. Winter sunlight streamed through the front windows, dust particles danced above the espresso machine. Lola was behind the counter, her dark curls wild as ever, dancing to Fleetwood Mac while she steamed milk.

"*Mon dieu*," Yves muttered, stopping just inside the doorway. His eyes traced the rounded curves of the bar, the precise angle where it became slightly uneven. He approached the bar and reached out to touch the wooden counter, his fingers running along the water rings.

"Yves! Finally!" Lola called out, breaking his trance. "I've heard so much about you that I feel like we've already met." She came around the counter to give him the traditional *bisous* but stopped short when she saw his expression. She asked if he was feeling okay.

"I'm fine," he said, shaking his head slightly. "Just...Was the bar always here?"

"Yes, I think so," I said, leading him to a corner table. "This place used to be a bar—the best one, same name too, well-known in the late '60s and '70s. We talked about it in Paris, remember?"

He nodded. "And the stage used to be on this wall?" he said, pointing across the room, excitement tangling in his voice.

Lola brought us two cappuccinos, the foam decorated with perfect hearts. "Yes, I think you're right," she confirmed.

"I had the same reaction as you when I found this place," I said, cozying up to him.

His eyes lit up, possibly relieved his sudden reaction was validated.

One evening, we took the Staten Island Ferry at sunset. The cold wind whipped off the harbor as we stood at the railings. Yves wrapped his coat around us both; I felt his heart beating against my back as the Statue of Liberty stood before us.

"She's French, you know," he whispered in my ear. I found him funny. He always had this effortless comedic timing too.

At *Kim's Video* on St. Marks, we rented old films—three by Louis de Funès. We created a nest of blankets on my floor and watched them on my tiny TV. Yves would translate the older French language I didn't grasp, his voice soft in my ear, adding his own commentary that made me laugh.

Later that night, we alternated between my beat-up CD player and his Walkman, playing our favorite songs. He had brought with him four cassettes: Hendrix, *The Best of Charles Aznavour 1976*, Dire Straits, and Nirvana.

We went to *Cafe Wha?* the next evening. I had never been there before Yves practically dragged me out that night. As we descended into the warmth of the club, we were hit by the smell of bourbon and leather; the energy of this club seemed frozen in time. Many people, dressed in true '60s fashion like us, danced in crowds and drank in couples—it was a "dress-on-theme" night. I stood, frozen on the stairs.

"What's wrong?" he asked, turning to face me.

My eyes were distant, searching. "No, it's nothing."

I knew the feeling. It had been happening more frequently—like when he'd adjust my necklace, or the specific tone his voice took when he called me '*ma chérie*.'

My feet pushed me forward and to the back booth. There was something about the back booth that always felt more comfortable: you could see everyone, but no one could see you.

Yves kept his hand on my knee, drawing absentminded circles with his thumb as the band played Rolling Stones covers; when "Wild Horses" filled the room, we fell silent—absolutely silent—for maybe half an hour.

We ordered whiskey neat, though neither of us usually drank it. The first sip burned. Yves kept looking at the stage, then the bar, then back to me, as if he was trying to piece together a puzzle with missing parts.

The whiskey glass trembled slightly in my hand as fragments of something—not quite memories, more like echoes—rippled through my consciousness. It was the way the light caught his profile, the specific angle of his slouch against the leather booth, even the chip in the wooden table beneath my fingers—like recalling a story I'd read before but couldn't quite remember the ending to.

The sensation was like trying to catch smoke—the harder I reached for it, the quicker it dissipated. But it left something heavy in my chest: an ache of recognition so profound it felt like grief.

Yves must have sensed something, because he squeezed my knee gently, breaking the spell.

"You look like you've seen a ghost," he said.

I almost laughed at how close yet far he was from the truth.

"Maybe I have," I whispered, more to myself than to him. Letting out a little laugh, chaos twinkling behind my eyes, I added, "Maybe I am one."

The band shifted into "Paint It Black," and something in the room's energy shifted too. Yves stood suddenly, pulling me to my feet.

"Dance with me," he said, though it sounded more like a memory than a request. The floor was crowded, but bodies seemed to part for us. His hand found the small of my back—the pressure, the placement, the temperature of his palm—all of it sang with frightening familiarity.

The smoke hung thick. Through the haze, couples danced, their clothes shifting between eras with each turn. I closed my eyes, letting the music and Yves's presence anchor me to the moment, but even the darkness behind my eyelids felt like an old friend. When I opened them again, Yves was watching me with an intensity that made my body come to a halt. The music softened and we stepped off to the side to catch our breath.

As the night deepened, we drank more whiskey, each sip feeling less like a choice and more like following a script. The burning had turned to warmth, spreading through my chest like oil to a fire. And that night, I cosplayed the girl who chose to pour gasoline over the fire, not water.

"Sometimes," he said, "I dream about a life like this. And you're always there, in that exact shade of lipstick."

Around midnight, the band played "Time Is On My Side," and Yves laughed—a sound so startling in its joy that several heads turned. "What?" I asked, already smiling, infected by his sudden lightness.

"Nothing," he said, shaking his head. "Just feeling lucky, I suppose." But the way his fingers intertwined with mine suggested he meant something else entirely—something lasting.

They say love is a choice, but we were more like muscle memory—a series of choreographed moves our souls remembered, even if our minds did not. We didn't try to explain the way time seemed to bend around us, creating pockets of *déjà vu* in dimly lit bars and airports.

—

On Christmas Eve, we cooked in my tiny kitchen. My parents were expected to arrive soon. The windows fogged up from the heat of the oven, creating a cozy barrier between us and the winter night. Yves insisted on making *raclette*, a dish common in French homes around Christmas time, filling my apartment with the scent of melting cheese, herbs, and butter.

I didn't have a *raclette* grill like every French home, so we made due with a small hot plate in the center of the table. Yves made me swear I would never speak of this back in France. He feared to be exiled by his friends and family. Completely dramatic, but I promised.

My parents liked him. They found him kind and smart. My dad said Yves had a good head on his shoulders. He said it was rare at that age to know exactly what you want in life—wanting to be a successful architect and design a beautiful home to share with a wife and dog; having a plan already was admirable, my dad said.

My mother, protective as always, liked him and said I found a true genuine spirit. She approved, but didn't elaborate much beyond that—trust came with time.

Later that night, curled on the couch, wine glasses empty and bellies full, I watched him in the glow of my Christmas lights, the colors painted across his face—flickering red, gold, red, gold.

Christmas morning arrived in silence, not a single car horn on the streets, only the radiator's gentle hiss in the corner. Yves traced patterns on my bare back, drawing his building floor plans into my skin. I turned to face him, grinning softly. He scratched away the crust gathered in the wrinkles of my eyes.

"What are you thinking?" he asked, his voice still rough with sleep.

"How moments become memories even as they're happening," I replied. "I'm already nostalgic for this morning, even though I'm still living it."

He understood. He always did.

"Write that down," he said, with a quick peck on the lips before throwing the covers off his side of the bed and sleepily walking to the shower.

After breakfast, we opened gifts.

He gave me a beautiful compact mirror in red crocodile-patterned leather, accompanied by a handmade brown tortoiseshell acrylic comb from Paris, my initials engraved small on the back.

In the same spirit, and coincidentally, I had a cover for his sketchbook made in black leather and his initials engraved small at the bottom. I had also knitted him a scarf and promised to spray my perfume on it before he left so a part of me was always cuddled into the small of his neck.

The days melted together. We created our own little world in my apartment, cooking, reading, making love. At night, I'd watch him sketch in his notebook, his hands moving with such certainty as he drew the city as he saw it—raw, romantic, alive. Sometimes he'd draw me too, always when I wasn't looking; I found sketches of me reading, sleeping, or lost in thought.

New Year's Eve arrived too quickly; we held an intimate party at The Fox with Lola and some close friends to watch *Dick Clark's New Year's Rockin' Eve* on TV. The café was decorated in gold tinsel and Christmas lights; it was nearly midnight, and everyone was tipsy.

"Ten... Nine... Eight..."

I pressed closer to Yves's chest, memorizing the feel of cashmere against my cheek.

"Seven... Six... Five..."

His arms tightened around me; time felt liquid, simultaneously racing and frozen.

"Four... Three... Two..."

"*Je t'aime*," he whispered against my temple.

"One!"

The world erupted in celebration, but our kiss was gentle, almost reverent. Lola grabbed the bag of confetti from behind the counter and threw it up in the air. It rained down like snow, getting caught in our hair and covering the entire floor—she really overdid it with the decorations, forgetting we would need to clean up before the opening shift on January 2nd.

In bed that night, the city still celebrating below, I watched him sleep. "You're staring," he murmured, eyes still closed.

"I'm remembering," I corrected. "For later."

The last days slipped through our fingers. We both became quieter, more desperate in our touches and kisses. Everything felt weighted by the realization of his impending departure. We headed to my film guy down the street to get our pictures developed before Yves left.

The morning he left, my apartment felt like a theater after the show—still humming with echoes, but somehow empty; his scent lingered on my pillows, and I found little traces of him everywhere: a forgotten toothbrush, his coffee mug in the dish rack, a sketch of the view from my window left on the desk.

At JFK, we held each other until the final boarding call. His heart hammered against mine, our rhythms syncing one last time.

"This isn't an ending," he promised, his voice thick. "Let's just say 'until next time.' It sounds better that way."

I'd been here before—last year, only it was in Paris, and I was the one boarding the plane.

I watched him disappear into the clouds, taking pieces of me with him; the drive home was a blur of unshed tears and half-formed poems. My apartment felt cavernous—too big and too small all at once. The weeks that followed were gray—not the romantic gray of Paris, but the hollow gray of absence. His letters, however, came regularly.

Then March arrived, bringing with it an unexpected revolution: AOL finally reached Europe.

AUDRIANA CRISTELLO

```
To: MatildaCherie

From: YValliere75011

Subj: For Matilda
```

```
Mon cœur,
I think technology has finally caught up with
our love...

This morning, I went to our island, Île Saint-
Louis. The morning fog was heavy, just like
that morning I brought you pastries in bed.

I had breakfast at that corner café - you know
the one with the red awning and wobbly chairs.
The waiter recognized me and asked where my
American girl was.

My coffee tasted bitter without you stealing
sips from my cup. The morning paper sat unread
because I had no one to translate the headlines
for. The chair across from me was empty, but I
could still see you there - hair messy from
last night, wrapped in my sweater laughing at
my terrible attempts at an American accent.

Je pense à toi,

Yves
```

The mechanical "You've got mail" became my favorite sound. We wrote about everything and nothing—his morning coffee, my latest projects, the way spring was arriving differently in our cities; instead of waking up to the chirping of birds, I wished for the *ding* of email notifications.

This was something new, something immediate.

Some nights I'd sit at my computer until dawn, watching our conversation unfold in real-time. It wasn't perfect, but it was ours, and for now, it would have to be enough.

Between classes, I found myself sketching more than ever. It was all so funny; I held it against my father because he insisted I was a fashion designer even after I repeatedly said I didn't want that. But there I was, drawing like one.

Yves had left his drawings scattered around my apartment —quick studies of building facades, my hands while I slept. They inspired something new in my work. My fashion designs became architectural—strong lines, sharp angles, an emphasis on structure I'd never considered before. I began drawing mindlessly, discovering my femininity and exploring a more gentle relationship with myself. I began to take care of myself: body scrubs, moisturizing before bed, nail care, replacing my linens with 100% Egyptian cotton.

I felt hopeful. My identity was flourishing and a woman sprouted in its place.

Meanwhile, in Paris, Yves's life was shifting too. His emails came at odd hours, full of exhaustion. A developer had approached him about overseeing permit applications and construction logistics for an office renovation at La Défense. It wasn't the creative design work he dreamed of, but it was a foot in the door.

"It's all bureaucracy and building codes," he wrote one night. "But I think of you when I'm there, looking out over the city from the 47th floor—mainly because I think of New York City, the Empire State Building and all that."

We were both busy, growing in different directions but somehow still tangled in each other's lives; we let each other become tangled though—intentionally and wholeheartedly. He began studying interior design beyond the structure, but the fabrics to use inside the building. He must have told me a million times that he wanted to design his own chair—an art piece for the living room, really. It reminded me of the furniture in my grandmother's sitting room: never to be used, just admired.

Some nights, between my deadlines and his early morning meetings, we'd catch each other online. The familiar *ding* of AOL would break the silence of my apartment, and suddenly the distance wouldn't feel so vast.

We'd write about our days, our dreams, the little moments we wished we could share. It was different from our letters—more animated, alive—but I still kept every letter he'd ever sent me, tied with a ribbon in my bedside table drawer, the paper soft from re-reading. I must have had over twenty of them, his first letter in December 1994 to his last, March of 1996.

DÉJÀ VU

To: YValliere

From: MatildaCherie

Subj: Matilda's Little Thoughts

Hi, sweet Yves,
I wanted to catch you before I slept for the night. Today, I started a new project: a skirt. Leather crocodile pattern - I got inspired by the compact mirror you gave me at Christmas time.

Um, I thought of something today. Wanted to share with you…

I have this tendency to listen to sad music, knowing damn well that I should just skip to the next song - a happier one to preserve my mood. But I can't. It's an art to feel. I don't want to skip one single moment to feel something because most of the time, we feel numb in this world. By the things we can't control or hell - even the things we can. So how? How could I possibly skip a song that has given me something real to feel.

I thought of that in the subway today, watching an older woman with headphones. She seemed to contemplate changing her cassette, but never did.

I know, a bit random to say, but I love to tell you things. Plus, I kinda felt the same about you. Knowing that something will bring you heartache but you do it anyway. And for good reason. I love you.

Matilda

11

June

His last letter lay crinkled between bills and notices on my desk; the pale blue envelope sat like a time capsule from another life. I opened it after one week. I couldn't get myself to open it and I wasn't sure why.

His familiar scrawl filled the page, ink slightly smudged from his left-handed writing, telling of newfound success. He left the band, Les Sauvages, for another rising band, one with greater potential to make international headlines—called Les Petits Rois, who he'd discovered playing in a cramped bar in the 11th arrondissement.

They were a group of four from Lyon—three brothers and a cousin—who'd moved to Paris with nothing but their instruments and a shared dream. Antoine, the eldest at twenty-two, had a voice that could charm angels, while his brothers

Marc and Henri played guitar and drums, and their cousin Thomas played bass.

"You would love them, June," he wrote. "They have that infectious energy, like The Beatles in their 'voyage to America' days. Antoine has that same fire you have on stage—that ability to make everyone in the room feel like he's singing just for them. They're rough around the edges but genuine. Pure."

Their sound was a perfect blend of '60s British Invasion and French pop; their lyrics, though French, carried universal emotions that transcended language. Claude had signed on immediately, becoming their tour manager after their previous one quit due to a family matter. Within three months, they were playing sold-out shows across France.

Their first single, "Dans Les Rues de Paris," topped the French charts for six weeks straight. Even people who didn't speak a word of French found themselves humming along. The music video was shot in black and white on the streets of Montmartre.

Claude was booking venues in Berlin, Amsterdam, and Madrid; his letter spoke of late-night train rides through the European countryside, of watching crowds fall in love with the band night after night, of finally feeling financially secure. He traded apartments for one much bigger. The tours were exhausting but exhilarating—six, sometimes seven months on the road, living out of suitcases and surviving on coffee and adrenaline while managing the band—who attracted different women in every city and smoked too many cigarettes. Claude turned in early every night and prayed the guys would show up on time for soundcheck.

"The other night in Brussels," he wrote, "I watched from backstage as two thousand people sang every word to 'Sous Les Étoiles.' Two thousand voices, June! I thought of you then, of how you always said music was the closest thing we have to magic. You were right. It is magic—pure alchemy."

Meanwhile, I was rising up on the New York scene; Atlantic Records had noticed my regular performances at *Cafe Wha?* too. Richard Palmer, a veteran A&R rep known for signing some of the biggest acts, had sat through three of the shows before approaching me. He'd watched from the back of the room, nursing a glass of scotch, taking notes in a small black notebook.

"You've got something," he'd said over coffee at The Fox one rainy Tuesday morning. "Raw talent, sure, but more than that. You make people feel like they're hearing their own secrets being sung back to them. That's rare. That's what we're looking for."

The contract sat on my kitchen table for two days while I agonized over every clause. Margot came over, and we read through it together, highlighting sections we didn't understand. I thought about calling Claude—he'd know what to look for, what pitfalls to avoid. He'd handled contracts for countless bands in Paris—but pride or fear or something else entirely held me back.

I signed my name in steady black ink on a Thursday afternoon. The moment felt both monumental and oddly anticlimactic—just a pen scratching paper, but it was the sound of my life changing direction.

The recording studio became a second home, a windowless room on 44th Street where time seemed to operate differently; days blurred together in a haze of coffee and cigarettes as we tried to capture lightning in a bottle. My producer, James Wilton —known for his gentle but persistent way of pushing artists to dig deeper, seeming to see right through people—was British and had a vulgar sense of humor. He was crazy, but it kept him inspired.

"Your voice has pain in it," he'd say, perched on a stool in the control room. "Don't hide from that. Use it."

So I wrote about everything: about growing up in New York City where the horizon stretched forever, yet with parents like mine, I never could escape past it; about my double life, which might possibly be exposed to my family with the album release; about loving someone across an ocean but forgetting their touch. The songs were just waiting for me to crack and pour all I had into them—some angry, some tender, some weak, but all of them honest.

One afternoon, after a particularly tiresome session trying to nail the bridge of another song, I sat alone in the studio with my guitar. The rest of the band had gone home, and James was on a call in his office. In the dim light, with my voice raw from eight hours of recording, I wrote "Letters to Nobody."

Time zones and tear stains
Paper planes crumble in rain
Your words grow fainter
Like footprints in foreign sand
The postcards pile up in corners
Of a room I can't keep clean
While you're chasing thunder
Through cities I've never seen

Chorus:
These letters to nobody
Pile up by my bed
All the things I couldn't say
All the words I left unsaid
Time makes strangers of lovers
Distance makes ghosts of friends
These letters to nobody
That's how every story ends

Remember how you held me
Like architecture holds the sky
Now memories turn sepia
And I can't remember why

DÉJÀ VU

I'm keeping all your secrets
In a box beneath my shame
Writing letters in my head
That never spell your name

Bridge:
The ocean grows wider
With every passing day
Your voice gets softer
As the dial tone fades away
I'm running out of paper
Running out of grace
Running out of reasons

James found me there, still playing the last chords over and over. He hadn't said anything, just pressed the record button. That raw first take ended up being the version used on the album.

Meanwhile, Claude's letter sat unanswered on my desk back home, gradually disappearing under bills, takeout menus, and show flyers. Days turned into weeks, weeks into months; the more time passed, the harder it became to pick up a pen. What could I say? Apologize for disappearing for half a year?

Everything I drafted sounded hollow somehow, insuffic-ient—most of all, selfish. I hadn't let myself focus on anything else but my art; he had a life, and it seemed a good one at that, yet I hadn't written back even to congratulate him. Writing a letter to apologize after all this time felt like throwing a dart in the dark and hoping it would stick.

Subconsciously, I questioned whether I had distanced myself to get some perspective—which I then used for my album. Was I that crazy? *That* dedicated to my career? Or simply, deeply, too independent?

I convinced myself that he was over me. His life in Paris seemed perfect—managing a successful band, traveling around Europe, finally doing what he'd always wanted. He was probably too busy to think about me. Maybe he'd met someone else, someone who could be there—present, real—not just a voice on a phone or words on a page.

But in all truth, I was certain he hadn't forgotten me; being on the road makes you think of everything you don't have—a warm and consistent bed, your favorite coffee mug, and that one girl who hasn't written in months or tried to contact you.

He was on the road. On the road for six, seven months at the least. It was an obvious remark, and yet I didn't quite put it together. It was possible he thought my letters were all sitting there, waiting for his return to Paris; perhaps, he expected dozens of them.

Nonetheless, I threw myself into the recording process, working fourteen-hour days until my voice was raspy and fingers were callused from guitar strings. The album was taking shape—a collection of songs tracing the geography of my heart, from childhood through teenage years to young adulthood.

The record label loved my look—a mix of retro and edge that felt authentic rather than manufactured. They wanted to shoot the album cover at *Cafe Wha?*, capturing the raw downtown energy that had first caught their attention. I insisted on using my own clothes, refusing their styling suggestions that felt too polished, too removed from who I was.

I wore a sheer cape that draped on the floor. It was a baby pink color with feathers that lined the trim. I wore black leather pants and platform boots. My bangs were styled to each side and raging with volume.

We got the final album cover after a few tries; I swung around the fabric of the cape to have this in-motion kind of shot. I held the microphone and sang "Time Is On My Side," the version from The Rolling Stones' second record. Felt too self-absorbed to sing a song of mine.

At night, I'd find myself back at my desk, staring at Claude's letter; I studied the photograph he'd included—him backstage with Les Petits Rois, all grinning after what looked like a triumphant show. Claude stood slightly apart, wearing that black leather jacket I remembered, his hair longer; I memorized every detail, afraid that one day I'd close my eyes and not be able to picture him clearly anymore. The photo helped.

Sometimes, late at night when the city quieted to a hum, I'd pull out our old letters, reading them chronologically like chapters in a story that had lost its ending. His words were still there, unchanged—stories about discovering bands in tiny Paris clubs, about morning coffee at Les Deux Magots, about missing my voice in his ear—but they felt distant now.

When my first single was released in October, I wanted to tell him; I imagined him hearing it on some radio station, recognizing my voice through the static. But all those months of silence felt like an ocean too wide to cross. Pride and shame had built a wall between us, brick by brick, letter by unsent letter. A wall I had constructed myself.

"Muse," my debut single, charted well. It felt like a miracle. Margot and I celebrated with champagne. And that night, it was decided: I didn't like champagne, and champagne didn't like me.

Suddenly I was doing radio interviews and photo shoots for music magazines; the success came faster than anyone expected. My parents found out through a neighbor on the elevator; my father wished he had a son interested in business instead of a rebellious daughter and my mother didn't shun me like I expected. She never explained why, and our relationship never changed. I was still welcome in my parent's house and at dinners if I wanted.

During the interviews, they asked about my influences, songwriting process, and the stories behind the lyrics. I talked about New York, even little tidbits of growing up in a strict household, but never about Claude. Never.

"There's something in your voice," an interviewer from *Fritz* magazine said. "A kind of beautiful melancholy. Where does that come from? Overseas, I'd imagine right?"

I smiled, feeling betrayed by the obviously intrusive question. I twisted the silver ring on my finger—a nervous habit I'd developed. "Sometimes the best songs come from the words we never say out loud," I replied. "The ones we wish we had the courage to say."

At night, when it felt too quiet and too loud all at once, I sometimes caught myself picking up the phone—I still knew his number by heart. But what time was it in Paris? Was he even home? The tours with Les Petits Rois kept him moving across Europe like a pinball, bouncing from city to city. I'd seen their name in music magazines, read about their growing success. They were being called the future of French rock. Margot reconnected with a friend in Paris, so I had an insider scoop from time to time about Claude's band too; Margot shared little words on the matter. She asked her friends and reported to me—no questions asked, even though I knew she had a million of them locked behind her sealed lips.

The months rolled on. My album was finished, and James said it was some of the most honest work he'd heard in years. The label was excited, planning an autumn release to coincide with a small East Coast tour—everything was falling into place.

I'd find myself humming "Letters to Nobody," thinking about the way distance could become a habit, how silence could grow roots, how two people could have everything and still feel incomplete.

Every Sunday, I'd sit down with fresh paper and good intentions. But the words never came out right. As a writer of songs and poetry—how could I possibly struggle to find words?

So Claude's letter still remained unanswered for eight months in counting, a ghost of what we'd been, while I sang my heart out in a studio on 44th Street, turning our story into songs that strangers would soon relate to, possibly more than we did.

The album, which we decided to call *Letters to Nobody*, was set for release in January 1967. Atlantic was confident in its potential, planning a proper promotional push. There would be a release party at *Cafe Wha?*—I had insisted on that, wanting to start where it all began; the show was already sold out.

Recording the final tracks felt like closing a chapter. Track nine was the title track, "Letters to Nobody"; James had fought to make it the lead single, but I refused. It was the last track on the album for a reason—it required the entire story; it wasn't the starting point. And it was too close to the bone. I wasn't ready for the radio to have this one yet.

The music magazines were starting to take notice. *Rolling Stone* included me in their "Artists to Watch" section—a small photo and write-up that deemed me *a voice for the lovesick and lost, for anyone who's ever fallen in love when they shouldn't*. I cut out the article and framed it.

December came, bringing with it memories of last year's shows. I heard through the industry grapevine that Les Petits Rois were huge in Europe now—their debut album had gone platinum in France, and they were starting to get attention from British labels. I imagined Claude in some European city, probably wearing that same leather jacket, charming everyone and making connections with important people.

Sometimes I'd catch glimpses of our life together in unexpected places—a French café on Thompson Street reminding me of our mornings, or the vintage store where he bought me that gold necklace, still my favorite piece of jewelry I owned—or had ever owned.

In January, I did a photo shoot for *Rave Magazine* following the album release. The stylist wanted to capture that "authentic downtown artist" look, so they shot in my apartment. I had carefully cleared Claude's picture from my nightstand before they arrived, hiding it in the drawer with his letters, but during the shoot, I kept glancing at the empty space where it used to be, like pressing on a bruise to see if it still hurt.

I wore the gold necklace for *Rave Magazine*—in every single photo.

At night, I often found myself on the fire escape, smoking cigarettes and looking at the city lights. New York had given me everything I'd wanted—a record deal, a voice, a future.

Maybe Claude was somewhere in Paris, standing on his balcony too, looking at the same stars and thinking about the letters we'd stopped writing. I hoped he might grab a copy of *Rave Magazine* and see the necklace staring back at him. It was stupid. All I had to do was call.

Before the photoshoot, the advance copies of *Letters to Nobody* arrived at my doorstep—it was November 1966, before the public release. Nine tracks. I kept one copy sealed, writing Claude's address on a padded envelope, but like all the letters I'd written, it stayed on my desk, unsent. I promised myself I would send it this month. I liked the idea of sending him simply the record—nothing else, like a gentle nudge, or peace offering.

And so I waited—simply, for nothing but the courage to walk down to the post office.

12

Matilda

The city was changing. I felt it in my bones as I walked down St. Marks Place that spring, past the kids in their newer, cleaner leather jackets. The edge was softening, like a photograph left too long in the sun. Even CBGBs seemed more like a tourist attraction than the gritty music venue of my teenage dreams. Times Square was being sanitized, brick by brick, needle by needle. The city I grew up in was transforming into something else entirely.

I graduated from Parsons in May 1997. My collection was well-received: a series of architectural pieces inspired by Art Nouveau buildings in Paris. I used lots of draping, creating organic lines that flowed like the ironwork of Guimard's *métro* stations. The centerpiece was an evening gown in midnight blue silk that transformed as the model walked, revealing hidden panels of silver lamé.

My parents attended the graduation show. Even my father seemed impressed, though he still asked how I planned to make a living designing pretty dresses. As a lawyer, he didn't quite grasp the idea of creativity as a viable career. Afterward, I caught my mother touching the fabric of my designs, a soft look in her eyes I'd never seen before. She was proud—just didn't vocalize it.

That evening, Lola threw a party at The Fox. We stayed open late into the night, drinking prosecco and dancing to Third Eye Blind. The song "Semi-Charmed Life" had been playing everywhere in New York that spring. It captured something about that moment—this sense of being on the verge of wanting more.

In late May, the news of Jeff Buckley's drowning hit us all like a punch to the gut. His music had been the soundtrack to countless nights at The Fox, especially "Last Goodbye"—though now the title felt too prophetic. Lola closed early that day. We sat on the counter where the old stage used to be, sharing a bottle of wine, playing *Grace* on repeat until our hearts ached less. "Remember when he played at Sin-é?" Lola asked, her voice thick. "God, he was beautiful."

I always loved that album—it felt like an extension of the '70s. You could have sworn you'd heard the cries of Zeppelin. I strolled around Central Park listening to it until the album ended, completely engrossed by his vulnerability and haunting voice.

I thought about how some voices become a part of our youth. And how losing them felt like losing an era of your life.

The summer after graduation, I landed an internship at Calvin Klein as a Fabric Development Intern. The position seemed almost too perfect, like the universe had saved this one for me. I remembered my first day vividly: walking through those glass doors on 39th Street, my heels clicking against the marble floor, trying to look as if I belonged there.

My desk was small, but I made it mine. I kept a stack of fabric swatches in one corner, organized by weight and texture. The other corner held a collection of coffee cups that grew steadily throughout the day. The work was detail-oriented and sometimes tedious, but I loved every minute of it. There was something meditative about cataloging fabrics and creating archive books of each season through texture and color.

That year, I became quite a denim hoarder. I loved Calvin Klein for many things and their denim was unmatched. I had accumulated maybe ten pairs within a few months.

—

```
To: MatildaCherie
From: YValliere75011
Subj: Late night thoughts

Ma chérie,
It's 3 A.M. here. I'm sitting on my balcony,
listening to the rain. The project at La
Défense is becoming more challenging. We
discovered asbestos in the walls today. The
whole timeline is pushed back and the client is
furious. Sometimes I wonder if I chose the
wrong path - if I should have stayed with
something smaller, more creative.

But enough about that. Tell me about your
fabrics. What did you touch today?

Je pense à toi,
Yves
```

I spent my days between the fabric library and the product development office, running swatches back and forth like some kind of textile courier. Each fabric had its own personality—the way it draped, the way it caught the light. I learned to identify weaves by touch alone, eyes closed.

I'd stay late, organizing the latest shipments of fabrics, creating detailed cards for each one: weight, composition, supplier, price point—everything had to be perfect. Sometimes I'd find myself lost in the task, looking up only to realize the office had emptied hours ago.

Every night, I would send Yves a nightly recap and respond to any emails he sent throughout the day. I could tell his days off from his working ones—limited to one or two emails on workdays.

```
To: YValliere75011
From: MatildaCherie
Subj: Update


My Yves,
Today I handled the most beautiful cashmere
from Italy. It reminded me of your camel coat -
the one you wore when we first met. Do you
still have it? I hope so.

The archive books are coming together. It feels
like I'm creating little time capsules of
texture.

Don't worry, you did choose the right path.
Just let life test you a little - there is
something to learn every time. Stay positive.

Miss you,
Matilda
```

His next email came two days later, shorter than usual. His father had been diagnosed with lung cancer, Stage 4. The news came like a hammer to glass—sharp, shattering. Robert, the artist who preferred to live minimally so he could spoil his children, who taught Yves to see beauty in imperfection, had three months, at best.

AUDRIANA CRISTELLO

```
To: MatildaCherie
From: YValliere75011
Subj: Dad
```

```
I don't know how to write this. The doctors say
there's nothing they can do. He's still
painting, and refuses to stop. Says he needs to
finish his last collection. I sit with him in
his studio sometimes, watching him work. His
hands shake now, but somehow the paintings are
more beautiful than ever.

I want you here. Is that selfish? To need you
now, after all this time? Can we plan a call
sometime this week? I need to hear your voice.

Yves
```

The world felt heavy after that. I threw myself into my work the next day, trying to speed through tasks I normally take more time and pleasure in. I told my boss that my boyfriend was having family troubles, and she allowed me to go home a few hours early.

That night, I sat at my computer, cursor blinking in the email window. I wrote to him and waited for his response.

```
To: YValliere75011
From: MatildaCherie
Subj: Re: Dad
```

```
My love,
It's not selfish. Nothing about grief is
selfish. It's about taking time for you. I wish
I could be there, sitting beside you in that
```

```
studio, watching your father paint. I wish I
could hold your hand.

Remember what you told me that day in Central
Park? About feeling too much being proof that
we're alive? You were right. Feel everything.
Even the pain. Especially the pain.

With time, things will hurt less.

I'm here. Different time zone, different city,
but here. I hope you read this soon. I would
love to call you tonight. Tell me if that's
possible.

Your Matilda
```

One evening, as I was labeling new fabric cards, my supervisor Margaret stopped by my desk. She watched me work for a moment, then said something that caught me off guard: "You know, most interns treat this like a stepping stone. But you-you treat it like it's your full-time job."

I looked up at her, this woman who'd spent thirty years in fabric development, who could identify a fabric's composition just by touch. She was impressive.

She smiled—really smiled—for the first time since I'd started. "Come in early tomorrow. There's a meeting with the design team I think you should attend."

The next morning, walking to work in the early summer heat, I thought about how life moves in cycles—birth, death, creation, destruction. In the fabric library, I ran my fingers over a piece of silk charmeuse, watching how the light changed its color from pewter to pearl and back again. Everything transforms, I thought. Everything changes—just have to be brave enough to let it.

Days at Calvin Klein blurred into deadlines and more deadlines. My French, once just a connection to Yves, became an unexpected asset. I found myself taking more calls from manufacturers in France, translating not just language, but cultural nuances that could make or break a deal.

I really couldn't explain how the language flew off my tongue. I studied and read for years, even before I met Yves, but it didn't quite make sense of how I grasped onto words I'd heard once and without question, retained for the next time. Yves was impressed.

And there is something so wonderful in impressing your partner; a peace sets over the body, and you really *can* celebrate something as a success. Or maybe it's just in my DNA to downplay any sort of accomplishments until someone brought in an outside perspective.

"Listen to how she handles the communication with Pierre from Lyon," I overheard Margaret telling another executive. "She understands when to push and when to yield. That's not something you can teach."

After a few months of conversation between the French suppliers and me, they began asking for me specifically. I was their first call when shipments were delayed or when they had new samples to showcase. Something about being able to understand their jokes and direct way of speaking made them trust me. I quickly became a bridge between the two offices, building a real trust.

While managing supplier relationships during the day, my nights were spent talking to Yves. The time difference meant catching him early in his morning, coffee in hand, voice still rough with sleep. Robert was declining faster than anyone expected. The doctors revisited their timeline; weeks now, not months.

Robert passed away on a Tuesday morning in September. Yves called me from the hospital, his voice hollow. "He finished the collection," he said. "Signed the last one an hour before…"

I pressed the phone closer to my ear, wishing I could reach through it, touch his face, hold his hand. "I want to be there," I said. "I should be there."

"No," he said firmly. "You're where you need to be. This opportunity at Calvin Klein—it's everything you've worked for. Dad understands that. He asked about you, you know."

My heart ached. His voice was haunted, tortured with pain and loss when he spoke.

We talked more about our future after that—not in the abstract way we used to, but with real plans, concrete details. He spoke about the house he wanted to design, spaces he wanted to create for us. "We're building something too," he said one night. "Just taking our time, making sure the foundation is strong, and waiting for the pieces to fall into place. When they do—when they will—one of us will relocate."

Nearly two months later, Margaret called me into her office. The afternoon light was golden, catching the fabric swatches spread across her desk. "Matilda," she said, gesturing for me to sit down.

"Our Paris office needs someone. They want a native English speaker who's fluent in French—someone who can be the communication point between New York and Paris, someone who understands both sides."

My heart stopped. Paris.

"It would be an assistant position," she continued, "but with real responsibility. You'd be helping manage relationships with our French manufacturers. The position opens in January."

I sat there, smiling, but unable to roll the words off my tongue. I was paralyzed, head-to-toe, with one simple feeling: hope.

Margaret grinned, the kind of smile that suggested she'd known all along. "Paris suits you," she said, "And so does that Frenchman of yours."

My mouth dropped. "How did you-?"

Margaret laughed. "You are not the only one who understands some French."

"I heard you explain that your French has advanced '*grâce à Yves*' on one of the calls," she added. "I figured you were speaking French outside of work too."

I thanked her, immensely and continuously. Nothing was confirmed yet, but she had really fought for me; she knew everything would fall into place if she did this for me.

—

The autumn light in the fabric library turned golden, then silvery as winter approached. I created my final archive book of the season, which Margaret reviewed with approval.

Without hesitation, she spoke, her voice somehow radiating off the brick walls. "I've already recommended you for the Paris position," she blurted out, running her hand over the carefully labeled swatches. "They're very interested."

I waited to tell Yves about the Paris opportunity. Not because I doubted his reaction, but because some news deserves more than a rushed phone call or hasty email. I wanted to choose the perfect moment, when the time difference felt smaller and the distance between us less vast.

Very early the next morning, I called him from my apartment. The city lights flickered outside my window as the phone rang. One ring, two rings, three-

"Matilda?" His voice was clearer than usual, more alive than it'd been for those past few weeks. "Everything okay?"

I curled up in my window seat and pressed the phone closer to my ear. "Everything's perfect, actually; I have news."

I told him about Margaret's offer—the assistant position in Paris. The words tumbled out in a mix of English and French. He stayed quiet, listening, until I finished.

"When?" he asked, his voice thick with emotion.

"January," I said. "If I get it. If they want me."

His laugh was soft, warm. "Of course they'll want you. You're exactly what they need—what we all need."

We talked for hours that night on AOL, planning and dreaming. He told me about morning walks along Canal Saint-Martin, about the best cafés for working; we'd be able to have coffee together in the mornings—real coffee, not just descriptions of it over email. The possibility felt enormous, terrifying, perfect.

Two weeks later, Margaret called me into her office again. The moment I saw her face, I knew; she was beaming.

"They want you," she said, sliding a formal offer letter across her desk. "The team in Paris was impressed by your knowledge of fabrics, but what really sold them was your understanding of both markets. They need someone who can translate *and* respect the language."

The letter was beautiful—thick cream paper with the Calvin Klein letterhead: Assistant Position, Fabric Development Department, Paris Office. January 15 start date. My hands trembled as I read the details.

"They're offering a one-year contract to start," Margaret continued, "And," she paused, smiling, "they specifically mentioned how impressed they were with your handling of the Lyon suppliers. Apparently, word gets around."

I signed the contract right then and there, my signature steady as ever; Margaret hugged me—the first time she'd ever done that.

That night, I called Yves again. When I told him it was official, he was quiet for a moment; then I heard what sounded like paper rustling on his end.

"I'm designing our home," he said frantically. "Have been for weeks, just in case. Want to hear about it?"

I pressed my face into my pillow, smiling so hard it hurt. "Tell me everything."

I liked that with Yves everything felt like it was moving forward—never a push and pull of commitment. We discussed our future home constantly; even though we both knew it would be years away before we could move out of the bustling city for our careers, let alone afford a house, we planned it nonetheless.

We talked for a whole hour, planning our life together in the city that had brought us together in the first place. We didn't even care about the phone rates per minute.

We would live in his apartment; it was a two bedroom, roughly 50 square meters with large windows and Haussmannian moldings. Everything was falling into place, piece by perfect piece.

13

June

The box stared back at me from my kitchen table—ten advance copies of the album arrived yesterday. Nine sat safely stored under my bed; one lay stripped of its shrink-wrap, ready to be packed. Eight months of silence lay between us, and I was going to break it with nine tracks of pure confession.

I scrawled Claude's address on the padded envelope with trembling fingers. No letter inside. No explanation. Just my vinyl.

The postal worker barely glanced up when I handed over the envelope; just another package among hundreds.

I lived in constant motion those following weeks: rehearsals ran late into the night, and press interviews blurred together, but my mind kept drifting to that package crossing the ocean.

The night of the release party came without any word from Paris. Someone had transformed *Cafe Wha?* into a twinkling dream: lights strung like stars across the ceiling, champagne poured into each glass. Music journalists mingled with the downtown crowd; I watched it all from backstage, heart hammering.

Margot found me first, slipping through the curtain. "Stunning," she said, tugging at my leather jacket; I'd worn it over silk—a nod to my old double life in this very room. "Though you look ready to bolt."

My laugh came out nervous. "I sent him the album."

"Finally," she lit a cigarette, the flame briefly illuminating her face. "When?"

"Four weeks ago." The words tasted like ash. "Nothing yet."

She blew smoke toward the ceiling. "Good. He's listening properly then."

Rob materialized behind her, all easy grace as he wrapped his arms around her waist. Something gold caught the light: a delicate, vintage ring on her finger. "You're engaged?" I squealed in shock.

Margot's smile could have lit up the room. "Last night. This fool got down on one knee at The Fox, right by the jukebox where I told him his band was garbage the night we met."

"She said we sounded like dying cats," Rob said, pressing a kiss to her temple.

"You improved," she leaned into him, still entirely herself, "Your band plays with June Eldridge, the star of the night; everything worked out."

The sight struck me. There was Margot—fierce, independent Margot—in love, without losing an ounce of herself. She hadn't disappeared behind Rob's shadow but had simply made space for him beside her dreams, her fire still burning bright.

My mother's face flashed in my mind—how she'd slowly faded into my father's world until I could barely remember who she'd been before. I'd spent so long terrified of that same fate. But watching Margot and Rob, I saw a future for myself.

The house lights dimmed—my cue; I shoved Rob off Margot and hugged her tightly. Rob ran out on stage and I waited for my name to be announced. My manager was meant to do it, but James had insisted it be him; he felt close to this album too, after all, as he was the only producer who had worked it.

The crowd roared when I took the stage; with the first chord, everything else vanished. I sang with my eyes closed, every word feeling more like a confession. When I opened them, I saw tears on a stranger's face. She got it.

Two days later, I was at Atlantic's office discussing tour dates with my manager. The hallway was the same as always: gray carpet, white walls, gold records in frames.

Then I heard it. Boots falling heavy on the floor, a rhythm I'd know anywhere.

I turned, and there he was.

Claude stood at the other end of the hall, still in that leather jacket, his hair longer, but the same length as in the photo he had sent me a year ago. He held a copy of my album in his hands.

The distance between us felt both infinite and microscopic.

"June," he said, his voice exactly as I remembered.

I couldn't move. Couldn't breathe. All I could think was how strange it was to see him here, in this hallway I walked every day.

He took a step forward. And then a few more. "The necklace," he said softly. "You still wear it."

I smiled softly; my lips parted and my shoulders relaxed at the sight of him, as if all the strength in my body ceased to exist. I tried to keep my composure.

"What are you doing here?" I managed to ask, my heart trying to exit through my throat.

"Les Petits Rois," he said, gesturing vaguely toward one of the conference rooms. "We're meeting with American labels. Atlantic's interested."

Of course. The universe had a sense of humor after all.

"I got your album," he continued, holding up the copy in his hands. It looked worn already.

I nodded, not trusting my voice.

"You wrote about us," he said. It wasn't a question.

"Practically every word."

He closed the distance between us then, slowly but deliberately. Standing this close, I could smell that familiar scent of leather and herbs—my Claude. His eyes hadn't changed—still intensely blue and seemed to see right through me every time.

"Why didn't you write back?" he asked, "After my last letter?"

"I was scared," the truth spilled out before I could stop it, "Of losing myself. Of loving you so much that my own dreams would fade away, that I would lose sight of my identity, my independence."

I touched the gold necklace at my throat. "But I was wrong. About all of it," I gulped, "I put my career first, but I should have balanced you both."

He noticed the necklace again, his fingers reaching out to brush against it. "You really do still wear it."

"Every day."

The hallway was silent except for the hum of fluorescent lights and our little voices. "I never stopped loving you," he said finally, "Even when the letters stopped. Even when I was touring Europe with the band, meeting new people in every city. It was always you."

"I never stopped either," I whispered, "The songs are proof of that."

He smiled then—that same smile that had first caught my attention at The Fox. "I know," he said, "I've practically memorized every lyric already."

A door opened somewhere down the hall. Voices approached; it felt like our time was running out, like we'd never say what we needed to be said unless it was right then.

"Les Petits Rois," I said, "They're really good. I've heard the imports."

"They are," he agreed. "And they want to tour America."

The implication hung in the air between us. A chance. A real chance. Or maybe a continuation of something that had never really ended.

"I have a tour coming up too," I said, "East Coast dates."

"I know." He smiled, "I read *Rolling Stone* magazine."

More voices approached; Claude glanced over his shoulder, then back at me. "Have dinner with me tonight," he said.

"Yes," I said simply.

He reached out, his fingers grazing my cheek. The touch was electric, familiar and new all at once. "I'll pick you up at eight."

I nodded. He turned away, headed down the hallway for his conference room.

I beckoned him back, my voice low.

"I love you," I said, disregarding all the engineers and managers shuffling around us.

He met my courage with an "I love you" in return. Then he was gone, his boots echoing down the hall, leaving me standing there with my heart racing and my skin tingling where he'd touched me. I pressed my hand against the wall to steady myself.

I caressed the gold necklace again, feeling its weight against my throat.

I thought about Margot and Rob, about how love could be a partnership rather than something that takes away your strength. I thought about my mother, who might have had her own dreams once. I thought about Claude, listening to my vinyl and packing it in his suitcase.

14

June

Chewing Gum

I never buy the silver packs,
not from shame or lack of means—
but for the thrill of being chosen,
for the warmth of others' generosity.

There are those who give
and those who wait,
a quiet division of humanity
played out in miniature.

Some carry abundance
in their pockets, ready
to bridge the gaps
between strangers.

While I—
I've made an art

of receiving,
a study in acceptance.

Perhaps it reveals
more than I care to admit:
how we sort ourselves
into givers and takers,

how the smallest gestures
become markers of who we are,
or who we've chosen
to become.

15

June

    I had been a taker for the last eight months, taking advantage of the love I had come to know, putting my career above all else. I waited for him to offer me a stick of gum.

    I had the initial thought—the one about the chewing gum—months ago, but I couldn't find the reasoning until Claude came back into view. I wasn't a defiant woman, but was growing into one. I wanted help but didn't ask for it. Wanted love, but didn't fight for it.

    However, in my career, I was not a typical kind of taker; I didn't take from others to get where I was—I did everything with respect and pride—but I had let myself fall out of connection with those who taught me those things. As much as Margot played into this tough character and nonchalant exterior, we hadn't spoken for one month, and I hurt her. I came to her apartment, wine and cheese in hand, and profusely apologized. She accepted.

"I knew you'd come around," she said, smearing her lipstick on my cheek. She told me that sometimes it's important to let someone roam, just to see if they'll come back to you.

"But I never understood why you let Claude go. What happened?"

I met her eyes with disappointment. "I was a taker; I took advantage of his love. Took my career and put it above all else."

Margot looked at me. "*Chérie*, trust me; you gave him a lot to think about before he left." Margot never lost that vulgar wit of hers. She always found a way to lighten the mood.

16

June

Dinner was at *Café Figaro* in the Village. I'd been there a hundred times before, but that night, the ambience between those four walls was different: the worn wooden tables felt different—softer to the touch, the surface so even under my fingertips. And maybe it was the way the candlelight caught Claude's eyes, or how his fingers tapped against his wine glass to the beat playing from the jukebox.

"So," he said, that half-smile playing on his lips, "tell me about the album."

I took a slow sip of wine, "You've heard it."

"I want to hear it from you."

The waiter brought our food: his *steak frites*, my bowl of mussels. The steam carried the scent of garlic through the air.

"It's everything I couldn't say in letters," I said finally, "Everything I was too scared to admit."

He nodded, cutting into his steak, "Track seven. 'Throw Me Around.' That's about The Peppermint Lounge, isn't it?"

"The night-" I trailed off, pushing a mussel around its shell, "When we danced with The Rolling Stones."

"I remember," his voice was soft, "Your lipstick was smudged for hours that night."

"You didn't tell me."

"I liked it that way."

"Yeah, well Mick got handsy while you weren't looking," I added, scrunching my nose with a smile so stupid and immature.

"You know, I saw Bob Dylan here one night; he was sitting in that booth—was the second time I'd seen him," I said, pointing toward a corner table.

"Did you say anything to him?" Claude inquired.

I grinned, brilliance in my eyes, and sipped my wine. "Actually, he came to me—said I looked like that girl in *Rolling Stone*. He thought my name was May."

"I said it was June and told him we had met at The Fox years ago; he told me he didn't remember, and I didn't hold it against him," I said, tearing into the bread, "But before heading to his table, he told me 'bye-bye magic eyes,' and I knew he remembered me."

Claude laughed, imagining Bob Dylan not being annoyed by my sharp tongue. "He's a pretty important artist, you know," I said, "Don't want to shit talk my way out of the music industry already by back-talking Bob Dylan."

The restaurant buzzed around us—couples chatted at nearby tables, waiters wove between chairs, the constant hum of Greenwich Village filtered through the windows—but we existed in our own pocket of time, suspended between what was and what could be.

After dinner, we walked without destination; the city was alive with Saturday night energy—music spilling from bars, teenagers lounging on stoops, the occasional car horn punctuating the air. We ended up at *Slug's Saloon* in the East Village, drawn by the sound of live jazz.

The band was good, real good; they were playing Armstrong and Fitzgerald's "Summertime" with a loose interpretation that made it feel jumpy, not too dragged out or sappy. The woman singing wore a beautiful sequined gown and had each man in the joint attached at her hip. Claude's hand found the small of my back as we made our way to the bar.

"Two whiskeys," he told the bartender, "Neat."

I raised an eyebrow. "Still drinking it that way?"

"Only when I'm with you."

The whiskey burned familiar paths down our throats; one drink became two, and two became three. The band shifted into something bluesy and slow, and Claude's hand appeared in front of me.

"Dance with me."

It wasn't a question, but then again, it never was with us. We moved by the current of the waves; we let our bodies carry us to the rhythm of the ocean, and I accepted his hand in mine.

His body remembered mine, and for a moment, I could pretend we were back at The Fox, that time hadn't passed, that we hadn't chosen different paths years ago.

"I miss this," he murmured into my hair.

"What?"

"The way you smell—like vanilla and cigarettes and something else I could never place."

I pressed my face into his neck, inhaling that familiar mix of leather and cologne, "You smell the same too."

Something possessed me that night; when the band asked for volunteers to sing, I found myself walking to the stage before I could think twice. As the first notes of "Fever" by Peggy Lee filled the smoky air, someone bolder, someone made of pure instinct, seemed to take over my body.

The room's energy shifted instantly. I found Claude's face in the crowd; he leaned toward the stage, watching me with pure wonder. Something in his gaze made me braver, made me lean deeper into the performance. I glided through the song I had sung a hundred times before. I loved the way singing jazz made me feel like an angel or a goddess—some unearthly creature.

When I hit the final note, the place erupted, the cheers feeling like a physical force. Claude met me halfway through the crowd, pulling me close. "Where have you been hiding that?" he whispered against my ear, his voice full of awe.

"Claude-" I said, starting to laugh, "I don't sing jazz, at least not outside of my shower."

A new band started their set just moments after; we swung each other around for hours, out-dancing all the other couples.

The final song ended, but we kept dancing until, at nearly four o'clock in the morning, we gave up. Outside, rain began to fall—soft at first, then harder. The sound mixed with the saxophone, creating a melody that felt like a memory I was already nostalgic about.

"Come home with me," I said suddenly. The words surprised us both.

His eyes met mine in the dark, "June…"

"Just tonight. Before you leave tomorrow, before reality comes back."

He answered by taking my hand in his.

The taxi ride was electric and entirely like us—chasing moments already lost; rain streaked the windows, turning the city lights into watercolor smears, while his thumb traced circles on my palm.

My apartment looked different with him in it—smaller, more intimate; I put on a Stones record, and "Going Home" filled the space between us. We shed our clothes at the door, left in only undergarments and socks. We danced around my apartment; the neighbors hit the walls continuously as we shouted "I'm goin' home, bome, bome, bome-bome-bome!" into each other's faces, holding invisible microphones. We were insufferably happy.

We didn't need words after that; our bodies remembered what our minds tried to forget—we had electric chemistry. His hands danced on my skin, and it felt like coming home and saying goodbye all at once.

Later, tangled in my sheets, we shared a cigarette and our truths.

"We could try," he said, watching the smoke curl toward my ceiling.

"Could we?" I propped myself up on an elbow, "You have Les Petits Rois; they're on the verge of something huge. You're traveling around Europe constantly. And I…"

"Have your album. Your tour," he said.

"Yeah. Here, in America."

The silence stretched between us, heavy with possibilities we couldn't quite grasp.

Morning came too soon, painting my bedroom in shades of gray; I watched him dress, each button of his shirt a countdown to goodbye.

The drive to the airport was quiet; different from last time, when we'd been full of promises and plans. Now, we knew better—or maybe we were just more afraid to abandon everything we'd created for ourselves.

At the security gate, he turned to me, "Write to me this time?"

I nodded, throat tight, "Every month."

"Liar," but he smiled when he said it.

His kiss tasted like coffee and regret; then he was gone, disappearing into the stream of travelers, taking a piece of me with him. Again.

I went home and put on Jefferson Airplane's "Blues from an Airplane." Grace Slick's voice filled the empty apartment as I sat at my desk, staring at a blank page; there were interviews to prepare for, appearances to schedule, an entire album to promote.

My manager called, "The *Today* Show wants you next week. And *Rolling Stone* needs those photos by Thursday for their new article."

"Okay," My voice sounded far away.

"You alright?"

"Yeah. Just caught me before my coffee."

In all truth, I was incredibly lucky that *Rolling Stone* cared enough to give me a second article—a bigger one. It was a feature about women making careers in music and climbing the charts.

The next two weeks passed in a blur. I did the morning shows to promote the album release, put on pretty clothes, and played my songs for rooms full of strangers. The radio stations wanted to dig up all they could about the songs; I gave them pieces of the truth but never the whole thing. I grew skilled at turning hard-hitting questions into cheeky jokes, never quite confirming my answers. I tired all my opponents.

The album was doing well—better than expected. My single, "Letters to Nobody," started climbing the charts, against my wishes but people liked it, I think, because it read like scribbles in a diary.

Margot helped me pack for Los Angeles. "You're brooding," she said, tossing another dress into my suitcase.

"I'm contemplative."

"Same thing," she sat on my bed, "Have you written to him?"

I shook my head.

"June."

"I know."

The flight to LA felt endless. Margot slept while I stared out the window, watching clouds pass beneath us.

Somewhere over Colorado, I pulled out my notebook and finally wrote to Claude. Later, in the hotel lobby, I sat pounding on the keys of the typewriter the concierge kindly let me use. I sent the letter the following day.

DÉJÀ VU

Dear Claude,

I've started this letter a hundred times since you left. Each time, my hand freezes over the page.

I want to keep us suspended in time - dancing to The Stones in our underwear, midnight sex, breakfast in bed. Nothing hurt. The truth is, I'm terrified of tarnishing what we have with promises we can't keep. Will you move to New York? Will I move to Paris? You love your job. And me, mine.

You asked me to write this time, and so here I am, thirty thousand feet above Colorado, finally finding the courage. Or maybe just finally accepting that some memories are meant to live in that space between reality and dream. Those moments are ours, ~~pristime~~ pristine and untouchable, even when we move in different directions.

I keep thinking about what you said - about trying. But maybe this is all we will ever be - we crash into each other like waves and then we retreat. You have your band, your tours across Europe. I have my album, a path to follow. But Claude, the way you kiss me makes me want to throw it all away sometimes.

I don't know what to do. We don't talk about the future anymore. I'm lost and I guess I'm wondering if you are too.

I'll send this before I can change my mind. Before I can convince myself that silence is safer than truth.

Always,
June

je t'aime
n' oublie pas

The Chateau Marmont stood like a castle on Sunset Boulevard; everything felt different there—the light, the air, even the way people moved. New York had edges; LA was all soft focus and palm trees.

Our room overlooked the pool, where film stars lounged like cats in the sun. At night, the hotel came alive with a different energy. Musicians and actors mingled in the garden, sharing cigarettes and secrets. I heard Jim Morrison was staying down the hall, though I never saw him.

The first time someone recognized me was at Whisky a Go Go; a girl with long dark hair and kohl-rimmed eyes stopped me between sets. She told me she liked my song "Con Man," and I thanked her—the words feeling strange in my mouth. I thanked someone for liking a song written about a man who never returned my admiration, but instead gave his to someone else.

I never understood why he hadn't chosen me when I so clearly chose him; I never received an explanation either—only saw the way he, even after choosing her, still watched my every move with sadness in his eyes, like he knew he had made the wrong decision but had to lie in the bed he made.

The Rascals played that night; the Whisky was chaos that night—pure, magnetic chaos. Bodies collided on the dance floor without apology, everyone too lost in their own moment to care who was watching. The music wasn't just loud, it lived in the walls, pounding through the crowd while the go-go dancers above us moved like flames in their cages, casting shadows below. Margot and I danced and drank before turning in early.

Later, in our hotel room, Margot found me out on the balcony, watching the Hollywood lights twinkle below.

"Different kinds of stars here," she said, joining me.

"Everything's different here."

She lit two cigarettes and handed me one. "You miss him."

It wasn't a question.

"I miss who we were," I said. "Before we knew better."

I sighed, "The vintage store, the dress I bought, the burgers we ate at Ruby's—we were young and didn't have much, just dreams."

"Maybe knowing better is overrated," Margot whispered, stroking my hair. "You're choosing practicality over passion, babe."

Below us, someone dove into the pool despite the late hour; the splash echoed through the courtyard, mixing with distant traffic noise.

I took a long drag of my cigarette, watching the smoke disappear into the night. "Maybe," I finally said, "But timing is everything, and I just might have missed my cue."

The next morning, I slept until midday; the city stretched before me, endless and bright. Somewhere across the ocean, Claude was probably just finishing dinner, maybe thinking about writing another letter. Time zones and responsibilities kept us apart, but maybe that was okay for now. We had our music, our words, our memories of whiskey-soaked nights and cab rides.

Sometimes love isn't about perfect timing; sometimes it's about holding on to the moments between the maybes, about dancing in dark bars, about writing letters that say everything and nothing at all. Acceptance.

I had interviews to do, songs to sing, a career to build—but I also had a letter to write, and maybe that was enough for now.

17

June

The road stretched endlessly before me, a ribbon of asphalt cutting through America. Cities blurred into a kaleidoscope of venues and faces. My voice grew stronger with each show, but an emptiness took its place in my throat. I felt alone and hardly spoke to anyone but a crowd.

The tour started intimately—in dimly lit clubs in Philadelphia where cigarette smoke clung to the velvet curtains, Boston basements where the ceiling dripped condensation onto the crowd, Baltimore venues where the floorboards creaked beneath my heels. But word spread. *Rolling Stone's* article had sparked something—a curiosity, a connection—and people wanted to hear these songs of love and loss, of distance and desire.

My tour manager, Jimmy, added more dates, bigger venues. "Your momentum is building," he'd say, dark circles under his eyes as he shoved another contract in front of me. "We have to strike while the iron's hot." His once-gentle guidance morphed into something harder, more desperate; the careful way he used to handle me disappeared.

By month three, I was playing to packed houses in Chicago—the *Aragon Ballroom* with its starlit ceiling and sweeping balconies—and Detroit's *Grande Ballroom* where The Who had played just months before.

Jimmy transformed into someone I barely recognized. He'd wake me at 3 A.M. in whatever city we were in, insisting I record song ideas before they slipped away. He booked last-minute radio appearances without asking, leaving me to stumble through interviews on two hours of sleep. "It's all part of making it," he'd say, but I wasn't sure I recognized what "making it" meant anymore.

Between shows, I'd find myself in dingy diners at dawn, drinking coffee that had gone cold while scribbling lyrics that felt forced. The waitresses would refill my cup without asking, their eyes full of either pity or recognition—I was never sure which.

The days began to bleed together—wake up in one city, perform in another, sleep on the bus to the next; my band tried to keep my spirits up—Rob especially was always ready with a joke or a story about Margot—but a hollowness was growing inside me that even their warmth couldn't touch.

Margot came out to visit me and reunite with Rob whenever she found the time. She had been busy lately, still working at the record label, helping a few artists compose and record.

I returned to New York for a brief week between legs of the tour. My apartment felt foreign, too quiet after months of constant noise. Margot waited for me there, along with three letters from Claude. I devoured them in chronological order, his words washing over me like rain.

AUDRIANA CRISTELLO

From his first letter:

```
Ma chérie,

I understand your fears because they mirror my own. How do we
build something lasting when our lives keep pulling us in
different directions? But maybe that's the point - we keep
getting pulled back to each other despite everything. Like
magnets, like gravity.

I heard your voice on the radio today. "Letters to Nobody" is
playing everywhere in Paris now. The announcer pronounced your
name wrong, and I wanted to call the station just to tell them
how it should sound.

I understand why you chose your career. I would have done the
same. We're both chasing dreams we've had since childhood. But
sometimes I wonder if we're not chasing the same dream from
different directions.

Your Claude
```

DÉJÀ VU

The second spoke of longing:

```
June,

I think of you every time I hear Stones on the radio. The other
day, "Wild Horses" played in a café and I nearly called you right
there. Time feels different without you - stretches and contracts
like elastic. Some moments feel endless, others slip away before
I can catch them.

Les Petits Rois played The Olympia last night. The energy was
electric - reminded me of your shows at The Fox. Antoine
dedicated a song to ill-fated love and I had to leave the wings.
Couldn't watch. Some things cut too close to the bone.

Paris isn't the same without you. Even the rain feels sadder than
usual.

Your Claude
```

AUDRIANA CRISTELLO

The third made my hands shake:

Mon coeur,

Les Petits Rois are recording now. Finally, I have time to
breathe, to think. Maybe too much time. All my thoughts lead back
to you.

The studio is in Montmartre, just down the street from Sacré-
Cœur. I walk up there sometimes during breaks, looking out over
the city. From that height, Paris looks eternal - unchanging. But
we know better, don't we? Everything changes. Everything except
how I feel about you.

The boys are creating something special. Their sound has matured,
grown deeper roots. Antoine writes about love like someone who's
lost it. Maybe we all have, in our own ways.

Your Claude

I called him that night, time difference be damned.

"*Allô?*" His voice was rough with sleep.

We talked about my tour extension—four more months on the road; he told me about the band's recording sessions, about finally having time to sit still. "It's strange," he said. "After all that movement, stillness feels foreign. Like learning to walk again."

The next leg took me west. Seattle greeted me with rain reminiscent of Paris—soft and constant, turning the streets into mirrors. The venue was an old theater with gilded mirrors and moth-eaten velvet seats.

Los Angeles felt like another planet entirely, different from when I was here last; it seemed like a city that changed its energy monthly. The *Troubadour* was packed every night, music executives gathered in dark corners, smoking cigars and trading stories.

I went out after my show, alone, looking for a moment of escapism. The Whisky a Go Go felt electric—as always. My eyes fluttered between open and closed as I threw my body around; I felt sexy, comfortable in my skin.

The tour continued on to places like Portland, Oregon, where the venue was well-worn, but the crowds were pure fire; Salt Lake City, where the promoter apologized for the small turnout, yet those who came knew every word; and Denver, where the altitude made my head spin, but the audience's energy carried me through.

Meanwhile, Jimmy grew more demanding. He scheduled shows back-to-back, leaving no time for rest. "The momentum," he'd say, as if it were some living thing we had to feed. "We can't lose the momentum."

I had a nightmare one night on the bus: Jimmy turned into a raging monster with bumps and lumps everywhere, skin that sagged and hideous facial features. "The momentum, June! The momentum," he said with a desperately ravenous tone. He lunged at my neck—angry, hunched over and hardly comprehensible. He ripped out my vocal cords and devoured them in front of me. I jumped out of bed, drenched in sweat, cracked the window and tried to fall back to sleep.

—

I wrote songs in anonymous hotel rooms, their walls thin enough to hear the couple fighting next door or the TV blaring down the hall. But the songs felt hollow, as if I were writing what was expected instead of what was true. My notebook filled with half-finished verses and crossed-out choruses.

The physical toll was obvious—my voice grew raspy, my eyes shadowed—but it was the emotional exhaustion that hit hardest: the constant motion, the endless parade of faces, the way each city began to feel like every other. I loved the support, but missed the intimacy of The Fox.

However, I blamed myself for these feelings; I had let myself become isolated. I didn't have Claude or Margot with me, but I had my band. Only Jimmy didn't give me the freedom to breathe, and I felt surrounded by his negative, demanding energy 24/7.

Near the end of the tour, I found Jimmy backstage, a bottle of rum in hand and leaning against a set of speakers. "Come here, beautiful," he slurred. "We have to celebrate your last show."

I stormed up to him, blood boiling. "Wipe that smirk off your face and the powder from your nose," I said, firmly. "You introduce me in five."

When I finally returned to New York—fifteen days later than planned, thanks to Jimmy's added shows—my apartment felt like a museum of who I used to be. One letter from Claude waited for me. Just one. I tore into the envelope, instant tears following as I read the letter three times.

```
My June,

I'm tired. We've been dancing this dance for years, and still,
we're no closer to being together. Every time I think we're
moving forward, life pulls us in opposite directions. I watch
other couples on the street - the simple way they exist in the
same space, and it aches.

I'll wait for one more letter from you. Your words - or silence -
will tell me everything I need to know. Maybe we're just two
people who loved at the wrong time, or maybe we're something else
entirely. But I can't keep living in this limbo.

I still love you. I probably always will. But love isn't always
enough, is it?

Je t'embrasse,
Claude
```

I grabbed the nearest paper and wrote back immediately, hands shaking. I sealed the envelope before I could second-guess myself and ran to the post office.

DÉJÀ VU

Claude,

Pick me up at Charles de Gaulle airport.

July 15th 1967.

flight 203 from JFK.

I choose you. I choose us.

yours June
♡

18

Matilda

My passport arrived in a large envelope, surprisingly light for something carrying such weight; I traced my fingers over my work visa. My photo stared back at me—an American, doe-eyed girl, nervous and excited all at once. Calvin Klein's legal team and HR had moved mountains to expedite the paperwork. Three weeks to departure.

My last day at The Fox was a blur. A regular customer, a man who had come in every morning for eight years, pressed a book into my hands—a worn copy of Sagan's, *Bonjour Tristesse*.

The evening before my flight, my mother appeared at my door unannounced. She carried a small, orange box.

"You should have this, dear," she said, sitting awkwardly on my bare mattress. "It was mine, in 1965."

Inside was a vintage Hermès scarf, deep burgundy with gold accents; the silk was soft with age, but still perfect. "I bought it in Paris," she continued, smoothing non-existent wrinkles in the fabric. "Before I met your father, I thought I might become a different kind of person entirely."

She paused. "My parents wanted me to marry a man who could take care of me. So, I found a rich man who could, but instead of having dinner with me, he had dinner with business clients and prospects on the horizon."

"And so I began to lose myself; a woman behind the man —careful not to take too much of his time, not too much of his energy. He needed it for work after all. It was his life, yet mine was somehow dwindling away."

I didn't know this version of my mother—the one who had gone to Paris alone, who had bought beautiful things just because they called to her. We sat in silence, the scarf spread between us like a map to another life.

"Don't let anyone dim your light," she said. "Not even for a millisecond—or you just might lose it forever."

I held my mother's hand, something I had never done before; she stayed for tea and helped sort through my clothes: pack, donate or leave for Lola.

The flight to Paris was long. I read fabric care labels in French—terms like *lavage à la main* and *repassage doux*— while the businessman next to me knocked back tiny bottles of alcohol.

Seven hours later, I followed the crowd through Charles de Gaulle, my carry-on thumping against my hip with each step. The airport hadn't changed—still chaotic, with shouting children and unclear signage.

Yves was waiting by arrivals, and something in my chest settled at the sight of him. He was beautiful in that effortless way of his, dressed in that cream cashmere sweater and dark jeans I remembered. When he saw me, his entire face transformed into that eye-crinkling smile I'd fallen in love with in the first place.

"I missed you," he murmured into my hair, his voice soft. He held me tight and dug his fingers into my back.

The taxi ride into Paris felt like a hallucination; everything seemed slightly off-kilter, like a dream where familiar things shift just enough to make you question reality. Yves sat close, our shoulders touching, but I found myself suddenly shy, unsure of what to do with my hands.

I watched his profile against the window, the way the morning light caught his cheekbones. He looked exactly the same and yet somehow different—more solid, more real than the version I'd carried in memory. His hand found mine among the luggage crowding our space, and I felt that familiar flutter in my chest.

Paris unfolded outside our window: gray stone buildings, zinc rooftops, patches of winter sky between Haussmannian facades. Last time I was here, I'd been running from something, but now I was arriving with purpose, with a future mapped out in work contracts and shared closet space.

Yves squeezed my hand as if reading my mind. We'd always had that—this ability to sense each other's thoughts without speaking.

"You're quiet," Yves said softly, his thumb tracing circles on my palm.

"Just taking it in," I replied, though it was more than that. I was overwhelmed by the reality of him—his presence, his scent, the way his knee pressed against mine in the cramped backseat. After months of dreaming about this moment, the actual experience was almost too much to process.

I remembered our first time here together—how young we'd been, how certain even then; that certainty had never wavered but had instead deepened into something more concrete. We knew, in our bones, that if we let this slip away, we'd never get it back—life moves too fast in the future's direction to revisit the past.

Later, in his apartment—*our* apartment now—I found evidence of how long he'd been preparing for this: a collection of Post-It Notes scattered throughout each room: "*Miroir*" stuck to the mirror and "*Le Dressing de Matilda*" on the closet doors. However, *Matilda's weird American measuring cups* were labeled for Yves. He had labeled everything so my mind would start compiling as many French words as possible in the first few weeks.

The bathroom made me laugh out loud; he had installed a proper shower head ("Because French handheld showers are barbaric," he'd insisted in his letters) and bought every French pharmacy product I'd ever mentioned loving. They lined the medicine cabinet, arranged by size like little soldiers.

That first week passed in a series of unexpected discoveries: learning that Yves sang in the shower—only Charles Aznavour, and only when he thought I was still asleep; discovering that my fabric swatches found their way into his architectural sketches—a scrap of silk pinned to a mood board, a swatch of wool used to test how light would fall in a space. Yves was starting to look for more interior design work, focusing less on the bones of the building and more on what made it feel like a living, breathing space.

My French improved in unexpected ways: I learned how to curse from the plumber who fixed our ancient radiator, how to sell from the flower salesman who saved peonies for me each week, and how to argue from the woman at the market who taught me how to pick the best produce.

Sundays belonged to us. Yves would wake early, as always, but instead of rushing to his drafting table, he'd stay in bed, tracing the lines of his latest blueprint on my skin. The morning light filtered through the sheer curtains, painting shadows across our tangled limbs. We'd make love slowly, deliberately, as if we had all the time in the world. After one particularly long week, I came home later than usual. Without a word, Yves stood up from his desk and walked toward me with arms open. I laid my suede jacket on the armchair, and we hugged. I had missed him. We lived together but never seemed to see enough of each other.

The apartment was dimly lit, a single lamp casting a warm glow across the room. I stood near the bed, loosening my hair from the pin that had held it up all day. I wore a sheer white blouse and jeans. Yves crossed the room in three quick strides, his eyes fixed on me, his black shirt slightly unbuttoned, revealing the edge of his chest. He looked better than I remembered—like seeing a familiar painting and remarking how beautiful it was.

He reached me, hands gripping my waist, pulling me against him. His fingers tightened. I felt the heat of his palms, the urgency in his hold. My hands slid up his arms, over the firm muscle beneath his shirt, and yanked the fabric open. He shrugged the shirt off, letting it drop to the floor, then grabbed the hem of my blouse. My bra was simple, black, and belonged to the floor now. My skin prickled in the cool air as he stared at my bare chest, his breath catching.

"Matilda," he said, voice rough, low. I didn't answer with words. My hands went to his belt, unbuckling it fast, the metal clinking as I pulled it free. His jeans hit the floor, and he kicked them away. I unzipped my own, shimmying them down. He pushed me back onto the bed, my hair fanning out onto the white linens. Yves climbed over me, his knees pressing into the mattress on either side of my hips. His hands slid up my thighs, fingers hooking into my panties, dragging them down and off. He shed his boxers next and pressed his lips hard against mine. Yves shifted, one hand sliding between my legs. His fingers brushed me, then pressed inside—two at once. My breathing turned ragged, loud in the quiet room. He pulled his hand away, positioning himself instead. My legs wrapped around his waist, heels digging into his lower back, urging him deeper.

My skin flushed pink as heat spread across my chest. He leaned down, his mouth finding my neck. I tilted my head back, giving him more, my fingers raking through his damp hair. His hand cupped my breast, thumb rubbing over my nipple, sending sharp jolts through me. The pace turned frantic. His thrusts grew deeper and I clung to him, my body tightening. It hit me first—pleasure crashing through me, making me shake, my cry muffled against his shoulder. He followed right after, a low growl in his throat as he spilled onto my belly. We collapsed together, breathless, tangled. He kissed my temple, soft now. I traced his jaw with my fingertips, feeling the faint stubble. We stayed like that, bodies cooling, the city's distant hum filling the silence.

The next morning, wrapped in his robe, I'd watch him in the kitchen. He had a ritual with the waffle iron—an ancient thing inherited from his grandmother, heavy cast iron that made perfect squares. The batter had to be just right and he insisted on doing everything himself. While he cooked, I would make our cappuccinos, their smell mixing with melting butter and warm syrup.

We developed our own language of intimacy: the way he'd press a coffee cup into my hands without asking, made exactly how I liked it; how I learned to read his body—the tension in his shoulders after a long day at the office, the way he'd soften under my touch. We'd eat breakfast at the table littered with my books, sharing sections of the *Le Monde* newsletter.

Some nights we barely spoke, communicating instead through gentle touches and knowing glances. Other nights we couldn't stop talking, sharing stories until dawn crept up on us. His hands would find mine in the dark, our bodies gravitating together as if it were the most natural thing in the world.

We weren't perfect—we had our moments of frustration, of misunderstanding, disorganization—but there was something solid beneath it all, a certainty that made even our arguments feel more like conversations than confrontations. My body didn't flare up into fight-or-flight mode; he didn't storm out of the room—didn't even move an inch. We simply figured things out.

The city changed with the January light—horribly dark some days, impossibly soft others. I watched it from our balcony, wrapped in my mother's Hermès scarf, thinking about the women we become when we allow ourselves to change. Below, Paris moved in its ancient rhythms, indifferent to my presence, but somehow making space for me anyway.

Work would start soon, bringing new challenges and rhythms, but for now, I existed in this in-between space: no longer a visitor, not quite a local.

19

Matilda

Calvin Klein's Paris office occupied the entire floor of a building near Place Vendôme; floor-to-ceiling windows flooded the space with natural light illuminating white walls and polished concrete floors. The room was sectioned off by nearly twenty workstations and racks of prototypes.

My desk sat strategically positioned between the fabric library and the design team's workspace—a deliberate choice by my supervisor, Charlotte. "You will be the bridge between the two," she had said on my first day.

I often stayed later studying fabric specifications, memorizing supplier information, and improving my technical French vocabulary. I kept a small notebook of industry terms, reviewing them on the *métro* ride home each evening. The early days were a whirlwind of new information every millisecond.

"I need the technical sheets for the Japanese denim," Charlotte called one morning, barely looking up from her sketches.

"The 13-ounce selvage or the stretch blend?" I replied without hesitation.

Charlotte's eyebrow raised slightly. "Both."

By the end of my first month, I could identify most fabrics blindfolded, running my fingers across the surface to feel the weave, the weight, and finish. The senior developers began seeking me out when samples arrived. I was seen. And quite proud of myself.

"This doesn't match what they promised," Michel, the menswear developer, muttered one afternoon, tossing a swatch on my desk.

I examined it carefully. "It's been mercerized differently. That's why the hand-feel is softer."

Michel nodded slowly and turned his eyes up to me. "She's got good eyes, this one."

Three months in, I'd earned their professional respect. The personal connections came more slowly, forged in small moments—bringing Charlotte her preferred *pain au chocolat* on deadline mornings, helping Michel find his glasses (always on top of his head), or making the Italian suppliers laugh with my imperfect but enthusiastic attempts at their language.

"Matilda," Charlotte said one Friday evening as the office emptied. "We're having a glass of wine. Join us?"

DÉJÀ VU

It wasn't really a question. Michel was already holding her coat, and we all walked together. We landed at their usual spot, a short walk from work.

We talked about everything except work, including Michel's divorce and Charlotte's daughter's newfound obsession with *Harry Potter*, the rising rents in Le Marais. They teased each other mercilessly and gradually included me in their quick-witted jokes.

Walking home that night, slightly tipsy and completely happy, I realized I had found my place.

—

In April, Yves found a painting in the storage unit where his mother had stored his late father's belongings; it was wrapped in brown paper, unmarked among dozens of finished canvases.

He unwrapped it at home while I was at work: a painting of two figures on a beach, their outlines barely sketched, the sky partially filled with stormy blues and grays; in the corner, two sets of initials—RV and YV—and a date: August 12, 1981.

Yves remembered that day: the wind had picked up suddenly, forcing them to abandon their painting session. His father had promised they'd finish it later.

But they never did.

I found Yves on the floor of our living room that evening, surrounded by his father's paintbrushes. The air smelled of dust and old paint. He sat motionless, his shoulders curved inward, looking smaller than I'd ever seen him.

"I was ten and got bored after an hour," he said, his voice hollow. "He kept saying we'd finish it someday."

That night, he slept restlessly. The next morning, he called in sick to work—then the next day, and the next. He barely spoke. He propped the canvas against the wall. The apartment grew quiet, almost reverent, as if the space itself held its breath around his grief.

I didn't push. I left for work each morning with a soft kiss on his forehead—softer than normal. I wrapped my arms around him more frequently, feeling his body gradually relax against mine. But I returned each evening to find him in the same spot.

Grief was contagious, I realized, but so was love. I sat beside him in the evenings, working on my fabric samples while he meticulously cleaned his father's paintbrushes. He cleaned my makeup brushes too and separated them on two different towels to dry by the window after.

On the fourth day, I came home to find him in the shower, the apartment filled with the scent of turpentine. The painting sat on an improvised easel by the window, catching the last rays of sunlight.

"I'm not going to finish it," he said that night, his head in my lap. "Life never stays suspended in time. Things change constantly, but the canvas doesn't have to. It'll stay as it is, forever."

He returned to work the next day, and the painting remained on the easel.

Three weeks later, Yves received a call from Jean-Paul, a hotel developer he had met at a networking event ages ago.

"I need someone who understands both structure and aesthetics," he said. "I've got a boutique hotel on Île Saint-Louis whose lobby needs a complete redesign. Are you interested?"

The hotel occupied a 17th-century building facing the Seine. Its lobby featured original stone walls and exposed beams, but years of neglect, mismatched furniture, and poor lighting had diminished its charm.

"I want it to feel like stepping into someone's private library," Jean-Paul explained, "but with the functionality of a hotel lobby."

Yves walked the space for hours, taking measurements, studying how the light changed throughout the day. He thought about one of his father's paintings—a woman's hands, delicately holding a book—and the deep reds and comforting moss greens Robert had used inspired him.

He envisioned custom furniture in contemporary fabrics, and warm lighting in yellow-orange hues: a table made from reclaimed wood for the concierge, antique brass fixtures for the doors and cabinets.

When he presented his concepts, Jean-Paul simply asked, "When can you start?"

Yves called immediately. "It's happening," he said, his voice higher than it had been in weeks. "I'm designing the entire experience, not just the physical space."

For weeks afterward, we spent our days off strolling through flea markets all over Paris, gathering vintage books, vases, and ceramic bowls to decorate the lobby.

—

I met Yves's sister, Aline Vallière, for dinner one evening. She was composed of grace, but had a ferocity to her madness. Her movements were deliberate and economical, yet never stiff. She embraced me warmly, kissing both cheeks with genuine affection.

"Finally, we meet," she said, her voice kind and steady. "Yves talks about you constantly."

She wore a simple navy dress with pockets on the front and bold silver earrings—minimal yet impactful. Her hair was lighter than Yves's and framed her face perfectly.

"The wine is decanting in the kitchen," Yves said. "I'll check on dinner."

Aline settled onto the couch, crossing her legs with natural elegance. "So, Calvin Klein. How is it going?"

I described my work, watching how Aline listened—fully present, nodding at exactly the right moments. Over dinner, I learned about Aline's work as a bank manager. She spoke about financial matters with remarkable storytelling ability, making international banking sound almost poetic.

"The trick," she said, popping a second bottle of wine, "is to take the work seriously without taking yourself too seriously."

I found myself hanging on every word, not just for content but for delivery. I noted how Aline punctuated sentences with subtle hand gestures, the slight raising of her eyebrows when brushing a topic off as ridiculous, the way she talked with a cigarette between her fingers—less like a habit and more like an accessory to her point, as if the cigarette itself were something of a defense to the argument.

After dinner, Aline suggested we go out. "There's this place by Canal Saint-Martin that plays jazz on Thursdays," she said. "Dancing is mandatory."

Her friends were already there and offered us glasses of wine upon arrival. She moved through the crowd with comfortable familiarity, introducing me to everyone. She was effortless.

On the dance floor, Aline transformed. She pulled me into the rhythm, guiding me through the crowd. "Don't think!" she called over the music. "Just follow me!"

I watched and learned, gradually letting go of my American self-consciousness. Aline danced with everyone and no one, completely present in the moment.

We met like this every Friday for weeks. I absorbed everything, piece by piece: I learned to defend myself in French by listening to Aline debate with friends, how to socialize easily by watching her interact with the bartender, and how to assert myself by observing her handle pushy men on the dance floor.

In June, for my 24th birthday, I had two birthday parties: one with work colleagues—more like friends now—and a *soirée* with family. My colleagues and I went out to a nearby restaurant in the 8th arrondissement with a beautiful terrace, the Eiffel Tower sparkling in our peripheral vision. We dressed in our best. We ordered a truffle pizza and a bottle of *vin blanc* (tell a French person once which wine is your favorite, and they will never forget). They were sweet, very human people. They gave me the perfume I had often talked about wanting and a heartfelt card thanking me for all the time I invested in the team and my work. I was touched. Beyond touched, actually.

The *soirée* with family—meaning Yves and Aline—was much different in pace; we went out and danced, drank wine until the sun came up, and slept through the entire next day. The wardrobe was casual: I wore slouchy trousers and a white tee. Yves was in a pair of jeans and a button-up. We looked polished but comfortable, exactly how all our *soirées* felt with Aline: easy.

20

June

I called Atlantic Records at midnight, knowing someone would still be working. My manager answered on the sixth ring, his voice rough with sleep.

"I'm going to Paris," I said without preamble.

"What the hell are you talking about? The album just dropped. We have interviews scheduled all week-"

"I'm going to Paris tomorrow," I repeated, my voice steady. "Call it a publicity stunt if you want. Musician goes rogue in Europe during album release. People love a rebel."

"June-"

"I've already booked the flight."

I hung up before he could argue. The tickets were on my nightstand. One way to Charles de Gaulle. I hadn't packed yet, but what did I need, really? Some clothes, my passport, the gold necklace that never left my throat.

Margot helped me throw together a suitcase at dawn, asking no questions until we were halfway through.

"Do you know what you're doing?" she asked finally.

"For the first time in years, yes."

The flight was eight hours of anticipation and doubt. I couldn't sleep, couldn't eat. The woman next to me kept trying to make conversation, but I couldn't focus on anything beyond the ocean we were crossing. Plus, she smelled so heavily of Chanel No. 5 that I felt partly suffocated.

What if he wasn't there waiting for me?

But somehow, I knew he'd be waiting, just as I knew I should have done this years ago.

I followed the crowd through passport control and baggage claim, heart hammering against my ribs. The automatic doors opened onto the arrivals hall, and there he was.

Claude stood in a shaft of morning light, taller than I remembered. His hair was shorter now, but his eyes—those blue eyes that had haunted my dreams—were exactly the same. He didn't rush toward me or wave; he just stood there watching, as if making sure I was real.

I walked slowly. Something about him looked different—steadier, perhaps. He had aged in the years since I'd seen him last, but it suited him—a man now, not the boy I had met at The Fox.

"You came," he said when I reached him, simple wonder in his voice.

"Well, I've wasted enough of our time writing stupid letters," I replied. "Was about time we tried the real thing."

His smile started slowly then took over his face. He didn't kiss me there in the airport; just took my suitcase and my hand, leading me toward the exit.

"What about your tour?" he asked as we walked. "Your album?"

"What better publicity than disappearing to Paris with the guy who inspired the album?" I said, laughing sarcastically from the back of my throat.

Outside, a taxi waited at the curb; the driver took my luggage as Claude opened the door for me. The leather seat felt cool against my legs.

"I have a surprise," Claude said once we were moving. "I found a place. On Île Saint-Louis."

"A hotel?"

He shook his head, a gleam in his eye. "An apartment. It's old, but beautiful. Fireplaces in every bedroom and a kitchen with these bright red tiles I know you'll like."

"An apartment," I repeated, the word settling like a promise. "For how long?"

"The lease is for six months, but…" He hesitated. "We could stay longer. If you wanted."

Six months. Half a year of waking up together, of coffee and arguments and make-up sex, of building something real instead of storing memories in envelopes and tape recordings.

Claude's fingers laced with mine as we merged onto the highway toward Paris. The morning sun caught his face in profile, gilding his features. I studied him openly now, noting the new lines around his eyes, the stronger set of his jaw. He explained he was letting Les Petits Rois go for this album's tour, handing them over to a new manager with connections in America.

"They're ready to fly," he said. "And I'm ready to stay in one place for a while."

"With me," I added. It wasn't a question.

His thumb traced circles on my palm. "With you."

"And if after this tour, they stay with the younger guy, that's okay too. I'll find another band." He smiled and said, "Right now, I'm going to enjoy the money I made from touring all those years."

"Hence the apartment," I said, upbeat.

"Yes, hence the apartment," he said. "Thought we deserved it."

I sat there, smiling like a child through my teeth. I leaned my head on his shoulder and closed my eyes. Peaceful. I felt peaceful. Shameful too.

The car picked up speed as we approached the city. Claude pointed out landmarks as we passed—the massive concrete business district of *La Défense*, the *Arc de Triomphe* in the distance. This would be my city soon; these streets, *my* streets. I tried to imagine playing small clubs here. The thought was terrifying and perfect.

"I have meetings set up for you," Claude said. "Small venues, people who owe me favors. You can play whenever you want, build something at your own pace."

The future stretched before us, suddenly tangible.

We were fifteen minutes from Île Saint-Louis when a truck ahead swerved suddenly, its back doors flying open. Our driver reacted quickly, but the car behind us didn't. The impact threw us forward, then spun us wildly across three lanes of traffic.

Time slowed. Glass shattered around us like confetti. The car folded inward, metal screeching against metal. I reached for Claude instinctively, my hand finding him in the chaos. I dug my fingers into his skin—something of a permanent engraving or tattoo.

Watching Claude's eyes roll back into his head, I might as well have already been pronounced dead. Seeing his beautiful face slowly drain of color and his body fall limp was more painful than the initial impact of the crash. My mouth hung open as I sobbed uncontrollably, my face pressed into his neck. Saliva fell from my mouth and tears from my eyes. I gripped the sweater he wore. It was the one he had left me with all those years ago and had slept with when I missed him. I had just given it back to him and there he was, dying in it. The car heated up and I couldn't find any strength to pull us out through the window. The car was completely crushed, and we were wedged in the backseat. I'm sure my legs were broken, but that's the thing about shock: the physical pain becomes irrelevant when the emotional pain is that great.

I was falling unconscious and growing too weak to cry any longer. I caught a reflection of my face in the window shards, just beyond Claude. My face looked further aged than it had just moments before—weathered, wrinkled, beyond repair, distraught. How was it possible to have aged so much in a matter of minutes? Heartbreak. Stress. Guilt.

I died with the face of someone utterly and completely disappointed by what fate had brought upon her. A 27-year-old face with lines around her eyes and sadness in her heart.

We had been so close to having it all.

All those years wasted—years spent crafting separate lives when we could have been building one together. I had made my career the mountain I was willing to die on, and now I was facing death from which there was no recovery, no getting back on track.

The cruelest joke wasn't the crash itself but its timing. After I finally chose love over ambition, the universe decided we'd made our choice too late.

I was struck by the absurdity of it all. My album would sell more copies now—*Tragic death of rising star June Eldridge in Paris with a mysterious lover. Was he the lover in all her songs?* They'd romanticize this moment, turn our blood into poetry.

But they wouldn't know how many times I'd sat at my desk, a blank page before me, choosing silence over reconciliation. How many times I'd picked up the phone only to set it down again—all because I was afraid of fading into someone else's shadow. But I had confused dependence with connection. I was caught in the momentum of the career I'd always wanted, realizing too late that Claude was all I ever really needed.

In our final moments, the universe granted me perfect clarity: I had always been more afraid of surrender than regret, and now regret would be the last thing I ever felt.

With Claude's body growing cold beside me, I understood that choosing someone doesn't mean losing yourself—it just means having a witness to your life; and I had denied us both that gift until it was too late.

June Eldridge 1940 – 1967
Claude Beaumont 1939 – 1967

21

Matilda

Yves's career transformed after the boutique hotel project on Île Saint-Louis. Word spread quickly, and suddenly the clients who had hesitated before were calling weekly—a restaurant in Le Marais, a concept store in the 6th, a writer's apartment near Montmartre that landed in *Elle Decoration*. Each project built on the last, creating momentum for the next.

His birthday came in September of our second year in Paris. His mother arrived with homemade brownies (Yves had never shown a liking to cake, even as a kid) and a yellowed envelope.

"I've been keeping this for you," she said quietly. "The note said to give it to you on your birthday."

Yves opened it later that night, after she'd gone. Inside was a letter scribbled in French, nearly 1,500 euros in cash, and bank account details. His hands trembled as he read it aloud.

DÉJÀ VU

My son,

If you're reading this, I've been gone for a while. I hope it's been long enough that the pain has softened. I sold *Red Morning* a few months before my passing—that big canvas from the blue period that you always said looked like a fever dream. Some American woman saw it at a showing I did and didn't blink at the price I listed it for. She had more money than sense, but I'm not complaining.

I've left you 10,000 euros in this account. Use it only to build something of your own—a studio, a firm, whatever your dreams are when you read this. The cash is for you and Matilda. Take her somewhere cold where you have to stay close. Create something that will outlast you.

Papa

That winter, we used the cash to spend a week in Chamonix. Yves was terrible at skiing but refused to admit it, insisting on the advanced slopes and ending each day bruised but laughing. We both remarked that he was a bad skier, but an excellent ice-skater however; how stupid of a thought. At night, we soaked in the hotel hot tub, planning Yves's future company between sips of *vin chaud*.

By spring, he had rented a small office space and hired his first employee—a recent graduate from his former school. Within eighteen months, Vallière Design had five employees and a reputation for creating spaces that felt both timeless and utterly contemporary.

My own career evolved more quietly; when Charlotte announced her departure—moving to London to oversee European operations—she recommended me as her replacement. At twenty-six, I became the youngest department lead in the Paris office.

My French was fluent now, not just technically but culturally: I could detect regional accents, catch subtle jokes, argue passionately about which television series to watch over dinner. I managed a team of four, traveling regularly to mills in Italy and Japan. The nervous American intern had been replaced by someone more authoritative—someone who wore chic slouchy suits with kitten heels, whose carefully trimmed bangs fell just above her eyebrows, who spoke softly but with absolute certainty.

With our increases in salaries, life expanded. We bought organic produce at the Sunday markets, invested in quality pieces for our wardrobes, traveled to Switzerland for long weekends just because we could. We weren't rich, but we were comfortable in a way that felt luxurious after our early days of budget-consciousness. We invested our money early in life, hopefully keeping our finances stable for decades to come.

Yves still worked late sometimes, and I still brought fabric swatches home, spreading them across our dining table while my tea grew cold, but we'd found a rhythm that worked—a balance of ambition and presence.

In December of 1999, just as the world buzzed with millennium anxieties, Yves asked me to meet him after work at an address on Île Saint-Louis. I assumed it was for a new project he wanted to show me.

The building was one of those classic Parisian gems—stone facade, wrought-iron balconies, a heavy wooden door opening onto a courtyard.

The apartment door was ajar when I reached it. Inside, the space opened to high ceilings, herringbone floors, and windows catching the last pink light of winter afternoon. The walls were bare, but the bones were perfect—crown molding, marble fireplaces, those tall French windows.

In the center of the empty living room stood a single round marble table with two bistro chairs—the kind you'd see outside a café; on the table sat a book I recognized immediately—Paul Éluard's poetry, the same copy Yves had been reading the day we met—and beside it rested a small black box.

Yves appeared from another room, hands in his pockets. "Surprise," he said simply.

"Is this...?"

"Ours. If you want it."

I crossed the room slowly, taking in the proportions, the light, the feeling of the place. "It's beautiful. But how-"

"Sit with me?" He pulled out one of the chairs, that familiar gesture that had charmed me from the beginning.

When I sat, he reached for my hand across the table. "Four years ago, you saw me reading this book and used it as an excuse to talk to me."

"Yves.." I said. "Are you-."

"I love you." His thumb traced circles on my palm. "The moment you entered my life, I knew I wanted to fall in love with you. You showed me the things I had forgotten to love. My creative side.. The beauty of small moments."

He opened the little box. Inside was a simple gold band with a single almond-shaped diamond that caught even the fading light.

"Will you marry me, Matilda?" he asked, voice steady.

When I said yes, something settled in me—a certainty that felt both new and ancient, like coming home to a place I'd never been before, as if we had finally reached the turning point in our lives where everything worked out.

We married the following May in a vineyard outside Florence; my dress was simple—floor-length crepe with a square neck and thin straps, the bodice structured just enough to create a slim silhouette—while Yves wore a chocolate-brown suit that made his eyes look greener than ever.

Our families merged easily: my father talked business with Yves's sister while my mother and his shared photos over prosecco. We took a few minutes to think of Robert too, throwing everyone into tears. I held Yves's hand up to my lips and tried to reassure him that he was there with us.

Later, when everyone had drunk enough wine to loosen their inhibitions, we danced under string lights as the Tuscan sky deepened to indigo; we even dabbled in the whiskey my dad had brought. At the end of the night, everyone, still a little tipsy, helped bring inside tablecloths, decorations, and music equipment. We took showers, and I made love to my husband that night.

The next morning, I woke up to Yves sitting up in bed, back against the headboard, reading. I curled up next to him, waiting for my eyes to adjust to the morning light. He held my vows, printed neatly on card stock. He smiled to himself. "Do you really think we'll find each other again?"

I smiled a knowing smile. "I'll be the girl drinking the whiskey," I said, laughing.

"Neat," he said. "Whiskey neat. Like the old days."

—

Yves,

From the moment we met, I began to see myself in a mirror created by you. A mirror that saw me as beautiful, graceful, and the woman you have been waiting for. You have given me the comfort to grow through phases rather than all at once; that human imperfection is something you encourage. For this I am grateful to you because I feel as though I am not only the woman you were searching for, but the woman I was too.

As you unfolded yourself to me, your existence only enriched my existing. To be loved by you is a feeling that will live within my soul for ages, but to love you has been my purpose from the moment we spoke. You found me in this life, I promise to find you in the next because I will always choose you. Support you. Admire you. And love you.

Yves Vallière 1971 –
Matilda Vallière 1974 –

A MESSAGE TO MY NEXT LIFE

About the Author

—

Audriana is an acclaimed author known for weaving intricate narratives that blur the lines between reality and fiction with a biography-style approach to fiction. With a unique perspective on storytelling, she creates immersive experiences that challenge readers to question where one memory ends and another begins—creating overlap in time.

Déjà Vu is her debut novel, inspired by her personal experience with unexplained connections, the malleability of time, and the power of second chances.

Audriana is an American author living in Paris with her husband—the man who deeply encouraged this novel and inspired it to life.

Message from me to you,

If you enjoyed my novel and find yourself with some time, please do leave an online review where you bought your copy of *Déjà Vu*. I appreciate you. ♥

Also, I've created a little playlist for you featuring all the music I listened to while creating the lives of these characters. Scan the QR code.

Audriana Cristello
www.audrianacristello.com

www.ingramcontent.com/pod-product-compliance
Lightning Source LLC
LaVergne TN
LVHW041927070526
838199LV00051BA/2732